THE BELVEDERE SCANDAL

Esther & Jack Enright Mystery
Book Eleven

David Field

SAPERE
BOOKS

THE
BELVEDERE
SCANDAL

Published by Sapere Books.

24 Trafalgar Road, Ilkley, LS29 8HH

saperebooks.com

ISBN: 978-0-85495-733-0

CHAPTER ONE

London, 1901

Tens of thousands lined the streets on a cold misty February morning to pay their last respects to the only monarch that most of them had ever known. Preceded by detachments of Household Cavalry, interspersed with ranks of infantry drawn from every regiment of the British Army, and with military bands playing music from every corner of the British Empire, the white ponies tossed their heads proudly. They were pulling the gun carriage on which was mounted the white-draped coffin that its occupant had specifically insisted upon.

After ruling England for sixty-four years, Queen Victoria was progressing for one last time past her former home in Buckingham Palace, then up Constitution Hill and through Hyde Park on her way to Paddington Station. Her coffin would be loaded onto the royal train that would convey it to Windsor Palace for the funeral service in St George's Chapel. Following two days of lying in state, it would then be interred in the Royal Mausoleum at Frogmore, alongside her beloved Albert, who had been waiting for forty years to be reunited with her.

Such was the fascination with which her loyal former subjects watched the passing gun carriage that they barely noticed those who followed solemnly behind it, among whom were her first-born, Albert Edward, now King Edward VII, and his wife of almost forty years, Queen Alexandra of Denmark. Almost all the senior members of the royal houses of Europe were also in this mounted column of mourners, not just because of their regal status, but because Victoria had been their mother, grandmother or mother-in-law. She had had nine children, all of whom had been married off to royal relatives.

Victoria had died a week previously in her beloved Isle of Wight retreat, Osbourne House, her oldest son by her side, along with the grandson who adored her, the German Emperor, Kaiser Wilhelm II. He had held her in his arms as she breathed her last, and had been one of those who had helped to lay out her body. He now rode solemnly alongside his uncle, the new king, in a rare gesture of family unity.

The entire route was lined with uniformed officers of the Metropolitan Police. In the lesser areas of the nation's capital it would be a good day to commit a crime, given that every available officer from the force was holding back the crowds of mourners who pressed close to each other, craning their necks for a good view. It had been the same wherever the royal coffin had travelled, first from Osborne House to Cowes, from where it had been conveyed across the Channel in the royal yacht *Alberta* to Portsmouth, with a flotilla of escort vessels alongside it containing the royal family. It had then been taken from Portsmouth to Victoria Station, where it had begun its final progress through the streets, lines of uniformed London bobbies bowing their heads in respect as the coffin passed them. Many of them had memories of three years previously, when they had restrained a more lively throng celebrating Her Majesty's Diamond Jubilee.

On both occasions, the responsibility for ensuring that there were sufficient uniforms on the ground for the purpose of preserving the public peace had fallen on the same man, Jack Enright. On the first of these he'd been specially detailed to conduct what was officially a survey of available manpower, but was in reality a cover for the more important task of smoking out a dissident group believed to be planning an attack on Victoria's life during the Diamond Jubilee celebrations. Now, at the elevated rank of Chief Inspector, he was the head of the Metropolitan Police's Manpower and Recruitment function within Scotland Yard. He'd not been home for a week as he supervised the rosters of those transferred from normal duties in order to line the public thoroughfares and hold back the mourners. This function would even cover the forthcoming events at Windsor, since policing of the royal residences there was also the responsibility of the officers.

Jack had spent the past few days in the control room on the ground floor of the Scotland Yard headquarters building in Whitehall. The room was equipped with several telephone and telegraph lines, to and from which urgent messages could be relayed from those outlying Met stations that possessed the necessary equipment. Fortunately, he'd not been called upon by any of them to send the reinforcements that he'd had on standby, waiting to be dispatched on the wagons that had been held ready in the courtyard outside. Shortly after five o'clock, Jack received the only message that he'd actually been waiting for — the one that confirmed that the funeral cortege had finally reached Windsor, and that everyone could stand down until the following day, Saturday, the day of the funeral service in St George's Chapel.

With a cheery 'Goodnight!' to the officers manning the communications channels with whom he'd shared the past few nervous hours, Jack walked into the chill of the darkening evening and took the horse bus north to his temporary residence in Hackney. It was the home of his Uncle Percy and Aunt Beatrice, the home that had also been his between the ages of fourteen to nineteen, when his uncle and aunt had taken him in after his father had died. The Enright family home in Essex had been deemed to be too far outside of London for Jack to pursue a career in the bustling capital. His mother had intended that this career would be in insurance, making use of the valuable contacts built up by his late father in his successful brokerage. But as Jack fell under the influence of Uncle Percy, a serving police officer in the Met, he'd been seized by an ambition to follow him. That had been twenty years ago, and his mother had never missed an opportunity to blame her brother-in-law Percy Enright for what she regarded as Jack's inappropriate choice of career, until her own death three years ago.

Percy had retired from the Met two years previously, but had rapidly discovered that an enquiring mind honed by regular exercise in police investigations would not settle for gardening and regular church attendance in the company of his pious wife. He had therefore opened what he chose to call a private enquiry agency, operating in two rooms above a candle shop a few streets away from his home. This had at first been Percy's little secret, until he'd volunteered his services to unmask whoever had been trying to force the closure of the private school in Watford of which Jack's wife Esther was the deputy headmistress. Percy's wife Beattie had resigned herself to the fact that Percy would be absent from what was meant to be his retirement even more often than he had been while still an officer in the Met.

Jack unlocked the front door, and was immediately assailed by the delicious aroma of roast beef wafting from the open kitchen door as he progressed into the dining room after leaving his outdoor coat on the hall stand. Since the infamy of Aunt Beattie's cooking was a long-standing family joke, he looked enquiringly at Uncle Percy, who was standing beside the dining table opening a bottle of wine.

'This will go well with the beef,' Percy commented with a broad smirk.

'If Aunt Beattie's cooked the beef, then presumably it's chloroform,' Jack joked, and Percy snorted.

'I won't tell her you said that. It's actually a very good claret, and it comes as a gift from a grateful client,' he informed Jack. 'As for the beef, it came from the cook-shop down the road. Not even your Aunt Beattie could ruin it, since all she had to do was reheat it while she murders the vegetables that will go with it.'

'So who was the grateful client?' Jack asked as he took his seat at the table.

'A wine merchant in St James's Street, who was losing stock at an alarming rate, but couldn't account for it on paper. His shelves were diminishing by at least a case of good stuff every week, but the books were square, and he was at his wit's end trying to work out how it was happening. So he called me in, and I had the answer by the end of the week.'

'Which was?' Jack asked, knowing how Percy loved to boast of his triumphs.

'It came down to carefully observing the daily deliveries out of the warehouse, which I did while posing as a temporary wine-taster. As you can imagine, that was no hardship at all. The first thing I noticed was that whereas the warehouse labouring staff worked alternating shifts, morning and afternoon, the warehouse manager was on duty all day.'

'The suspense is killing me,' Jack muttered sarcastically as he nodded in response to Percy's silent gesture with the opened wine bottle, and watched while his glass was filled.

'Well, clearly that opened up the possibility of a double delivery but a single entry,' Percy beamed, then looked disapprovingly at Jack's blank expression. 'Do I have to spell it out for the benefit of a senior Yard officer? The manager arranged for two deliveries to the same West End hotel, twice a week, on Mondays and Fridays. The first one went through the books, and the second didn't. The afternoon shift workers had no idea that the morning workers had already done the first delivery, and of course the paperwork was left to the manager. Then I arranged to travel with the second delivery, and was told by the banqueting manager of the hotel that it was the second that day. It was then a simple matter of finding out who, at the hotel, was responsible for the wine order. When I confronted the under manager with what I'd learned, he made a full confession in return for me not advising either the authorities or his employer. He and the warehouse manager at my client's business premises had been sharing the proceeds when the second delivery was collected by a rival hotel at half the going rate.'

'Pretty obvious, when you know how it was done,' Jack observed.

Percy nodded. 'But I only got to know how it was done by using my eyes, ears and brain, and bearing in mind that the best frauds are the ones conducted with barefaced effrontery right under your nose. Keep it simple, and maintain a smile at all times.'

Just then Beattie entered carrying the meat, and issued an instruction to Percy to collect the vegetables from the kitchen. 'And don't steal any on the way in,' she added.

'They'll probably give themselves up anyway, like all defeated opponents,' Percy replied.

'He doesn't get any better, as you can hear,' Beattie told Jack as she pulled a face. 'Anyway, how did things go in the city today?'

'Perfectly,' Jack told her. 'The only arrests were for pick-pocketing and groping in the crowded throng, and there were no riots or fatal crowd surges. Her late Majesty is safely at Windsor, the funeral service tomorrow will be a private family one, and then she'll be lying in state until Tuesday, when she gets buried. I thought I'd head off home for the day tomorrow, returning late for two more nights here, if that's in order.'

'Of course, dear boy. Remember me to Esther and the children, and tell her that we miss them all.'

'Of course, and perhaps when all this pompous nonsense is over we might have you all over for Sunday lunch,' Jack said with a smile. 'Although I doubt if we could run to a magnificent roast like this one,' he added, tactfully omitting to mention that he knew that it had been professionally cooked by hands other than hers.

As the early morning train clattered through Harrow on its way from Euston to Watford the following morning, Jack noticed that there were light snow flurries flickering past the carriage window. By the time they reached Bushey it had become a regular snowfall. As he waited outside Watford Station for the horse bus to take him down St Alban's Road to his home alongside the entrance to Cassiobury Park in Rickmansworth Road, he was brushing thick flakes off his overcoat and hat. It had clearly been snowing here for some hours, to judge by the slush tracks being churned up by the few wagons that were passing up and down.

As he walked carefully through the inch-deep snow at his front gate, he called out to his two youngest children, six-year-old Miriam and five-year-old Tommy, who were starting to build a snowman outside the front door. They looked up, gave cries of glee, then skidded towards him in their outdoor boots in order to give him a hug.

'We building Mr Frosty!' Tommy announced proudly.

Jack smiled as he replied, 'I can see that. Has Polly given you a carrot for his nose, and two onions for his eyes?'

'And then what would be left for the nourishing soup we were planning to have for lunch, in order to combat the cold?' came the challenge from the front door, where Esther stood beaming. She wore an old bonnet that was keeping the falling snow from her long black locks, now greying in places to acknowledge her thirty-sixth year. Jack hurried forward and gave her a big hug and kiss, and she ushered him swiftly indoors.

Once inside the house, he shook the remaining snow from his coat onto the mat by the front door, and hung his hat on the rack before following Esther into the sitting room. The all-purpose maid, Alice, had lit a roaring fire that nine-year-old Lily was hogging as she sat sewing a new dress for her best doll. Her younger brother Bertie was seated at the table, drawing up plans for an imaginary attack by his toy soldier cavalry on the enemy fort defended by infantry whose painted tin livery revealed them to be Coldstream Guardsmen.

'Hello, Papa,' said Lily, smiling up at him. 'I hope you're home next week, because Annabelle and I would like to go to the travelling fair in the park, and Mama says we can only go if you're with us, because the fair people aren't very nice.'

'That's not quite what I said,' Esther assured Jack, 'but obviously a travelling fair can attract quite the wrong sort of people, and for that reason the school won't be going. But if you can arrange to be free on Thursday or Friday, you could accompany the two girls. Annabelle hasn't yet lost her enthusiasm for circuses.'

Annabelle was a good friend of Lily's, and her love of circuses had nearly been her downfall almost two years previously, when she'd allowed herself to be coaxed into running away to join one that was performing in nearby St Albans. The devious influence behind that had been her stepfather, one of a small group of people in the pay of a more evil man whose ambition was to ruin the school at which Annabelle and Lily were both pupils, and of which Esther was the deputy headmistress. The man had sought revenge against the school's proprietor and headmistress Emily Allsop, for reasons that only Esther had been made privy to.

Although Annabelle had been safely recovered, the aftermath of the resulting police investigations had left her an orphan. Since she had been befriended by Lily, Esther and Jack had provided her with a new home until she could make her own way in the world. When she'd first come to live with them she'd been shy and withdrawn, almost sullen, because of her experience under the baneful influence of a demeaning stepfather. But she had gradually emerged from her shell, and was now a happy and grateful member of the Enright household, and a fitting companion for Lily. She sat on the carpet alongside her, reading a book in the warmth from the fire.

'If Lily and Annabelle get to go to the fair, then I want to join the Boys' Battalion,' Bertie insisted, and Jack turned to Esther for an explanation.

'I was going to mention that once you'd settled back in,' Esther responded. 'It seems that the Earl of Essex has been going round the local Board schools, recruiting for some sort of boys' army training outfit. Most of Bertie's friends have been granted permission to join, and I can't really see any harm in it, so I was hoping that you'd give *your* permission.'

'He's only nine years old, for goodness' sake,' Jack protested. 'Why does the old fossil need to recruit boys of that age for his pretend army of what I believe are called "Chocolate Soldiers" by some people?'

'I have no idea,' Esther replied, 'but bear in mind that the earl is our near neighbour, and we rely on him for his forbearance and tolerance when the children play in his park. He's an officer in the local reserve regiment, and takes his military role seriously. Obviously, boys as young as Bertie and his school friends won't be engaged in any sort of fighting, or even pretend fighting, and it'll be good regular exercise for him, rather than moping around the house playing with his toy soldiers.'

'I suppose there's no obvious harm in it,' Jack agreed, 'until the day they stick a broom handle in his hand and tell him to pretend that it's a rifle or something.'

'Thanks, Papa!' Bertie yelled enthusiastically.

'Did I say yes?' Jack demanded with mock severity.

'I think you just did,' said Esther. 'Now, are you hungry? I meant what I said about soup for lunch — and Polly's baked some of your favourite bread, the stuff with real grains in it.'

'After Aunt Beattie's cooking, I'm ready for something wholesome, but please don't tell me what's for dinner, because I have to get back to Hackney. I have another few days ensuring that Windsor is properly policed during the lying in state and the actual interment in the mausoleum at Frogmore.'

'When will you be home again?' Lily asked as she looked up hopefully from her sewing.

'Thursday — don't worry. Then we'll go and see that fair,' Jack assured her.

'I'm glad I swapped my stepfather for your Papa,' Annabelle whispered to Lily, who looked up at Jack with a grin.

'Did you hear that, Papa?' she asked, and Jack nodded as he held back a forming tear and Esther leaned sideways to plant a kiss on his cheek.

After leftover cold beef and freshly murdered vegetables on Sunday evening back in Hackney, Jack had an early night, and the following morning he took a relatively uncrowded horse bus down to the Embankment and Scotland Yard, where he reported back to the Control Room and enquired whether events had gone smoothly during the funeral service in St George's Chapel, Windsor.

'Nothing to concern us,' Sergeant Bullivant told him, 'although the Artillery chappies got a bit of a red face. It seems that the horses on the gun carriage started playing up, and had to be quickly unharnessed before they overturned the coffin that was already loaded on it ahead of the climb up the hill to the chapel. Anyway, some naval bigwig arranged for a bunch of bluejacket tars to get inside the harness and haul the carriage up the hill by hand. There was a bit of a scuffle in the officers' mess later, when the naval types started making horse noises in front of some artillery blokes, but their own Redcaps took care of that, and we had a peaceful night. And by the way, Bruce wants to see you as soon as you get in. I didn't see you, if you want to get a mug of something first.'

'Thanks, Jimmy,' Jack replied as he made his way to the canteen that served all ranks inside the Yard building, although no-one above the rank of Inspector had ever been reputed to frequent it. Armed with a mug of hot chocolate and a bacon sandwich, he took a seat in the far corner, where he was least likely to be spotted by anyone sent to look for him, and wondered what further annoyance Assistant Commissioner Bruce might have in store for him.

As the most senior officer in the Yard with overall responsibility for operations, Bruce was Jack's ultimate boss. He normally had little direct contact with him, unless it was for Bruce to express his discontent regarding the way in which Jack was discharging his duties. Since the security arrangements for the royal funeral procession had gone according to plan, and the remaining two days of the process were not open to the public, Jack could not think of any reason for an urgent response to Bruce's request for a meeting. He was hoping to catch up with some routine paperwork before returning to the control room to receive confirmation that all the extra uniformed bobbies that he'd allocated to the processional route had returned to their home bases. Then, after two more nights in Hackney, he was planning on taking two days in lieu of the weekend that he'd just forfeited, returning home in time to keep his promise to Lily and Annabelle.

He therefore uttered a loud groan when he looked up to see Constable Gormley, Assistant Commissioner Bruce's messenger and general dogsbody, standing on the other side of the table, looking down at him apologetically.

'You were sent to look for me, weren't you?' Jack sighed.

Gormley nodded. 'Sorry and all that, but the old man's really got his braces in a tangle over something or other. I don't think you're in trouble, if it's any consolation, but my best advice would be to get up there without delay, sir.'

'Tell him you found me in the control room ten minutes ago, which is almost the truth,' Jack told him, making a mental note to never again trust in the diplomatic silence of Jimmy Bullivant. Gormley agreed and walked away, while Jack swallowed the last of his hot chocolate, left the remains of his now cold bacon sandwich for the rats that were rumoured to have colonised the kitchens, and made his way up to the third-floor suite of offices from which Assistant Commissioner Bruce ruled his dominion.

'Ah, Jack — thank you for responding so swiftly,' Bruce beamed as he waved Jack into the visitor's seat in front of his desk. 'Congratulations on a job well done regarding that funeral show. Now, about the coronation that may or may not follow.'

'My legal knowledge doesn't stretch to constitutional matters,' Jack frowned, 'but surely there can be no doubt about that? The Prince of Wales is the firstborn of the late queen, and has been recognised as the heir for his entire life. He's already being hailed as the new king, and the coronation is just a formality, designed to show him off to his people.'

Bruce frowned. 'So everyone thinks. And indeed we've received confirmation from the Earl Marshall that the date has been set for the twenty-sixth of June next year, so you might want to make a note of that. But that's not what I've called you here to discuss.'

Jack waited politely as Bruce fiddled nervously with the pen in his hand, then looked back up.

'That man who made such a superb job of ridding the East End of Max Moses — the man who may or not be your Uncle Percy?'

'Yes, what of him?' Jack asked as he suppressed a smirk. The man in question had indeed been Percy Enright. He'd been grudgingly paid a thousand pounds by way of a bearer bond to protect his true identity, in order to suppress the dominance of Russian immigrant gangs who'd been all but holding the East End hostage. Percy had achieved that by means of inspired, but entirely underhand and devious, conversations that had set one rival gang against another, almost to the point of extinction. He had crowned that by persuading the leader of the most powerful of those gangs, Max Moses, to leave the country.

'We need to call on his services again,' Bruce announced with obvious reluctance. 'I need to set up a meeting between this man and Superintendent Melville of Special Branch. And I mean either today or tomorrow, such is the urgency of the matter. If the man of your acquaintance is indeed Percy Enright, then so much the better, because he's the man Melville would prefer, and seemingly they've had successful dealings before, during that Diamond Jubilee scare.'

'It might help if I knew why,' Jack replied.

Bruce nodded towards the open door. Jack took the hint, rose from his chair, closed the door and sat down again. Then, in little more than a whisper, Bruce said, 'We've had certain information, from a reliable source that we cannot even think of ignoring, to the effect that Prince Albert Edward may not be an appropriate person to occupy the British throne.'

'But surely, given his birthright and heritage as the firstborn…?' Jack objected, to which Bruce responded by slamming his hand down on the desk top. Jack jumped and left his objection unfinished.

'Clearly the man is qualified by birth,' Bruce conceded with obvious irritation. 'But it's more a matter of his personal character.'

'I know that he has a bit of a reputation as a playboy,' Jack ventured.

Bruce shook his head vigorously. 'Would that it were *only* that! If anything, that makes him even more popular with the masses.'

'Then *what*?' Jack demanded.

Bruce lowered his voice to the point where Jack had to lean across the table and strain his ears in order to hear the answer. 'Would the people be prepared to welcome him as our new king if they knew that he'd murdered two people?'

CHAPTER TWO

'Was Bruce drunk at *that* hour of the morning?' Percy demanded when Jack had filled him in.

Jack shook his head. 'I don't think I've ever seen him more sober,' he assured him. 'So are you free today, or preferably tomorrow? I don't see any obvious signs of frenzied activity in here, and your man on the front desk was staring into space as if looking for something to inspire him into action.'

Jack had known better than to seek out Uncle Percy at home, given that it was late morning. He'd instead walked from Hackney Station, along Mare Street, and into the narrow network of streets that led to Percy's business premises above the candle shop. He'd been given a mug of tea, and the offer of lunch down the road in Percy's favoured hostelry, before he'd even succeeded in stating his business, and now Percy was intrigued.

'Who is he alleged to have murdered?' he asked. 'Presumably the husband of his latest conquest in the bedchamber?'

'There were allegedly two of them,' Jack reminded him, 'and we won't know any more unless we make an appointment to see Melville.'

Percy made a rude noise as he recalled his first meeting with the Head of Special Branch. 'I'm surprised to hear that the old reprobate still has a job, given the way in which he conducts business, ignoring the rules and behaving as if he has carte blanche to do whatever he thinks fit.'

'I'm reminded of the old saying about pots and kettles,' Jack goaded him, given that Percy was known for his frequent disdain for the Procedures Manual.

'This was different,' Percy insisted as he recalled the way in which Melville had arrived in a coach, accompanied by a serious-looking operative called Reilly. Both of them had been armed, and insistent that Percy accompany them to the country residence of the Home Secretary. There he'd been inveigled into a counter-intelligence operation launched in order to thwart a threatened assassination of the queen during her Diamond Jubilee celebrations.

'*Why* was it different?' Jack challenged him.

'That time I was the victim, kidnapped from my own garden at gunpoint and forced to have lunch with the Home Secretary.'

'I can't believe you're serious,' Jack chuckled. 'Since when did Percy Enright object to a free lunch?'

'I don't see why you're regarding all this as some sort of joke,' Percy complained. 'You've just informed me that our king is a double murderer, and that I have to renew a *very* unsatisfactory working relationship with one of the most dangerous police officers I've ever known — one who, let me remind you, dragged *you* into that same business!'

Jack frowned as he remembered being obliged to become an undercover member of a subversive club bent on assassination, while Esther had ended up being kidnapped by her own brother. 'I hardly need reminding,' Jack grumbled. 'And, as I recall, one of those who we suspected at the time of subverting Met officers was none other than the man who's summoned us to meet with Melville — Assistant Commissioner Bruce.'

'He came out of that smelling of roses,' Percy replied with a grimace, 'but he must be pretty desperate if he wants me back on his team, officially or otherwise. Was there any mention made of how much he's prepared to pay me this time?'

'He's not entirely certain that you were the man he paid *last* time,' Jack reminded him, 'but we're walking around the important issue. Are you prepared to meet with Melville or not, and if so, when?'

'I have a few accounts to send out, and a report to write to a lady client, confirming that her intended does indeed have an illegitimate daughter by his previous conquest, but apart from that I can probably find a brief window of time tomorrow morning — at ten, shall we say?'

'May I use that telephone on your desk?' Jack asked, and a few minutes later he'd made the necessary arrangements. Then he reminded Percy that he'd promised to accompany him to have lunch at a local pub.

'Oh yes, well remembered,' Percy replied with a smile. 'Make the best of their hotpot, if it's on the menu today, because when you return to the Enright residence this evening, Beattie's threatened to cook one of her fish pies. It's what the local church minister of whom she's so fond would no doubt describe as "The Piece of Cod that Passeth All Understanding". You may well giggle now, Jack my boy, but you'll need that sense of humour when you meet with Melville again tomorrow.'

'I *knew* it was you!' Bruce crowed at Percy the following morning as he and Jack took two of the three vacant seats in front of his desk. 'And to think that I gave you a thousand, after all the trouble you caused me during your service days.'

'You clearly considered it money well spent, to be rid of Moses,' Percy retorted.

'Well, I won't argue with that. Incidentally, I'm advised that he recently made it across the water to the States, which suits us here in London even more than the little boat trip you organised for him across the Channel. Anyway, this time even you will find what we have lined up for you a considerable challenge.'

'I haven't accepted the job yet,' Percy reminded him, 'and there's the little matter of my fee.'

'What are your daily rates?'

'That rather depends upon the nature of the enquiry, and you'll appreciate that this is the first time I've been called upon to investigate a double murder by a reigning monarch.'

'An *alleged* double murder,' Bruce corrected him as he cast a nervous glance towards the closed door. 'Your job will be to prove the Prince of Wales innocent of these scurrilous allegations.'

'If they're scurrilous, why do you need me?' Percy asked, and what had previously been the hint of a smile faded from Bruce's face.

'The allegations come from the German Ambassador von Hatzfeldt, who's threatening to go public with them if we proceed with the coronation planned for June of next year. The Home Secretary is obviously beside himself, and the Commissioner has assured him that we can prove the allegations wrong. He's obviously called in Special Branch, and in a few minutes you'll be briefed by Superintendent Melville, with whom you are obviously already acquainted.'

'I look back on our previous relationship with the same pleasure as my most recent visit to my dentist,' Percy replied sourly.

'Personality clashes are not to be allowed to get in the way of a successful outcome to this business, do you understand?' Bruce said seriously.

'That won't be a problem,' Percy assured him with a cold smile, 'since Superintendent Melville has no personality worth talking about anyway.'

Bruce appeared to be framing a suitable retort when there was a knock on the door. It opened, and Constable Gormley's face appeared in the gap. 'Superintendent Melville's here, sir.'

'Good,' Bruce replied. 'Ensure that the door is firmly closed once he's admitted, and no-one is to approach closer than twelve feet from it once it is — yourself included. Now show him in.'

'Do you wish me to leave, sir?' Jack asked.

Bruce shook his head. 'No — this will involve you as well, given that your uncle's no longer on the force, so stay where you are.'

The door opened again and in walked Melville, a man in his early fifties who more closely resembled a society undertaker than a senior police officer. He had a bristly dark moustache streaked with grey drooping over a thin mouth, and a long spare frame draped in a charcoal three-piece suit, with an unfashionable high collar beneath which was a grey cravat. He smiled down at Percy as he took the seat between him and Jack.

'We meet again,' he remarked to Percy.

'The pleasure is entirely yours, believe me. At least on this occasion I wasn't summoned here at gunpoint,' Percy responded.

'There was clearly no need for that,' Melville replied lightly, determined not to be provoked. 'Once again the nation has need of your dubious services, because playing by the rules would likely get us nowhere.'

'And do you come with the authority to negotiate the fee for my unique talents?' Percy asked.

'How much has Bruce told you of what's involved?' Melville asked.

'Enough to know that for once in my career I'll be required to prove someone's innocence, and that the person in question has an entire nation's Treasury at his disposal,' said Percy. 'Is this when you assure me that I can name my price?'

'It merely reinforces my opinion of you, that you seek to put a grubby price label on something as vital to the nation as an orderly succession of monarchs,' Melville replied coldly, then turned towards Bruce. 'Before this descends into an exchange of insults, may I be assured that this loose cannon can be trusted?'

'As much as he ever could,' Bruce replied, 'but perhaps when he hears what's at stake, he may choose to be more patriotic in his outlook.'

'Very well,' Melville agreed, then looked meaningfully at Jack. 'What about him?'

'We'll clearly need to involve a senior serving officer to cover for the other Enright, and they've worked together well in the past, so please feel free to continue.'

'On that understanding,' said Melville as he looked first at Jack, and then Percy, 'be prepared to be shocked to the core by what I have to disclose. If you have any questions, please reserve them for when I've finished.'

'Agreed,' Percy replied.

Melville took a deep breath and cast his eyes towards the ceiling. 'During the last grouse season — in October of last year, to be precise — Prince Albert accepted an invitation to attend a hunting weekend at Bradenham House in Buckinghamshire, the country estate of Sir Rupert Belvedere and his American-born wife Virginia. She's at least twenty years his junior, and still starkly attractive, in that somewhat handsome way of American women. Sir Rupert is your typical "fading English gentry", living on a diminishing fortune amassed by his late father in the steel industry, supplemented by his wife's inheritance as the only beneficiary of the trust established by her late father's engineering endeavours. You get the picture, I imagine.'

'Loudly and clearly,' Percy growled, and Jack was reminded of his uncle's ingrained Socialist principles.

Melville gave him a disapproving sideways look, then continued, 'On the Saturday evening, after a very successful shoot on that first day, the menfolk remained in order to smoke cigars and drink unconscionable quantities of port and brandy, while the ladies withdrew to the sitting room to indulge in coffee, petit-fours and society gossip. Once the men were suitably past the threshold of sobriety, talk — perhaps inevitably — drifted towards the ladies and their physical attributes. I pause for a moment in my narrative to advise you, should you not already be aware, that Prince Albert has an appalling record for seducing the wives of his social companions. The Princess Alexandra seemingly turns a blind eye to his philandering, and those who regard themselves as blessed to have been granted membership of what we know as the "Marlborough House Set" are well aware that diplomatic silence is a condition of continued membership. We obviously have our own man inside Marlborough House, which was the prince's main residence until he recently transferred his corpulent self to Buckingham Palace following the death of his mother. Why are you grinning, Percy?'

'Your obvious distaste for what you're describing mirrors my opinion of our so-called "social superiors",' Percy explained, 'and you deliver it with a sardonic literary flourish that I appreciate. But I suspect that what you have to relate will soon become less amusing.'

'If I ever get there,' Melville replied reprovingly. 'Anyway, although we have our man in Marlborough House, he was not present at this weekend shooting party. We are therefore obliged to rely on the account of someone who is hardly likely to be well disposed towards the licentiousness of the English aristocracy. Be that as it may, it transpires that during this alcohol-fuelled bout of carnal boasting, someone suggested to the prince that he could probably no longer remember each individual occasion on which he'd bedded a lady of quality. Albert insisted that not only did he remember every dropped garter and every undone set of stays, but that he could probably identify each occasion in terms of the time, date and hour of the day.'

The phone on Bruce's desk rang at this point, and the flow of Melville's narrative was halted while Bruce picked up the receiver, rammed it back down on its cradle, then walked to the door and bellowed through it to Constable Gormley to divert all his calls until further instructed. He retook his seat behind his desk with an apology and an invitation to Melville to continue.

'Where was I?' Melville asked.

'"Every dropped garter and every undone set of stays," as I recall,' Percy replied.

'Yes, indeed,' Melville confirmed, slightly red with embarrassment. 'Anyway, quite how they got to the important point in all this I'm not sure, but the prince eventually agreed on a wager that he could identify every woman he'd ever had simply by their perfume, or the touch of their skin. Not only that, but that he could do so blindfolded. There were several ladies in the adjoining sitting room who qualified as former conquests of Albert's, so it was agreed that he would withdraw to his bedchamber, allow himself to be blindfolded by the valet assigned to him that weekend, and then identify the lady who was sent in. It was also agreed that, in order to make it harder for Albert, the lady in question might not necessarily be one he'd bedded.'

Percy and Jack exploded with laughter.

Melville gave them a withering look, then continued, 'Anyway, it seems that the plan went ahead. Albert went to his bedchamber and was blindfolded by the valet — a man called Wilson — then sat and waited. Meanwhile, one of the male party left downstairs was obviously in a provocative frame of mind, because he suggested to the host, Rupert Belvedere, that the lady sent into the prince's bedchamber should be his own wife, Virginia. This was highly sensitive stuff, seemingly, since Sir Rupert had his suspicions in that regard, but it occurred to him that this would be a God-given opportunity to discover whether or not Albert could identify her as someone he'd once bedded, and perhaps recently. So Rupert called his wife into a vacant room on the ground floor and put the proposal to her. She claimed to have been reluctant to engage in anything so — well, so *vulgar* until her husband reminded her that her reluctance might give rise to a certain inference, so she agreed.'

Melville paused briefly at that point in order to draw breath, and Bruce took the opportunity to offer him a mug of tea.

'No, that's quite all right, thank you,' he assured Bruce. 'I'm getting to the important part of my narrative.'

'We were wondering when that might happen,' Percy muttered.

Melville shot him an angry stare before continuing.

'I almost omitted to mention a curious feature of all this, namely that Belvedere, in his eagerness to persuade his wife to take part in this unseemly charade, suggested that she be blindfolded herself when she entered the Prince's bedchamber, and that he would need to be the one to guide her footsteps once she did so. We believe that the reason for this was to give him the excuse to hear what transpired between her and the prince, such were his suspicions.'

'And she agreed?' Bruce asked.

'She did indeed agree, and the two of them entered the prince's bedchamber. What happened next is what has given rise to the potential constitutional crisis that we now face. Those remaining downstairs, where the menfolk were about to be reunited with the ladies, heard two loud gunshots from the bedchamber. Several of the men and women rushed upstairs and burst through the door, where they found Prince Albert, *not* blindfolded, but looking askance at two bodies lying on the floor. One of them was Sir Rupert, and the other was the valet, Wilson, both of them dead from gunshot wounds. On a side table was the prince's own revolver — a standard Webley with five chambers — and three chambers of it were empty. Subsequent tests left little doubt that it had been the one that had fired the fatal shots, but the prince was unable to explain what had happened, claiming only that he'd heard two shots fired immediately after Lady Virginia had entered the bedchamber. The lady herself was hysterical, and had to be taken from the scene by several of the ladies who had raced upstairs when they'd heard the gunshots, but who remained outside the bedchamber in case the prince had undressed, which as it transpired he had not.'

It fell silent, and Percy looked meaningfully at Bruce as he restricted his question to two words. 'Local police?' he asked.

Bruce nodded. 'The Buckinghamshire Constabulary were contacted immediately, and an Inspector Darrow was despatched, along with several constables. Their conclusion was that the two dead men had killed each other in a duel arising from aspersions cast on the moral character of Lady Virginia.'

Percy gave a derisive snort. 'Is it time for questions yet?'

'Yes,' Melville conceded, 'but keep them brief.'

'I'll restrict myself to one,' Percy replied. 'How did we come to be meeting here today, all but accusing Prince Albert of a double murder, if the local force was satisfied with that somewhat bizarre and unlikely explanation? Or was it contrived because of the identity of the likely suspect?'

Melville sighed. 'Regrettably, one of those present that weekend, and a witness to the grubby wager itself, was a German industrial chemist called Otto von Huber. He was, at that time, a close business associate of Sir Rupert's, and was working with him on potential new steel smelting processes. Unfortunately, he seems also to be highly regarded at the German Embassy. We've subsequently conducted a few discreet enquiries regarding his connections with the German Emperor Kaiser Wilhelm, who is of course Albert's nephew. To cut a long story short, von Huber contacted the German Ambassador, who in turn called on the Home Secretary, seemingly at the behest of the Kaiser, to suggest that the local police were engaging in a whitewash, and that perhaps we here in England should think twice before allowing Prince Albert to take the throne as King Edward the Seventh.'

'May I be allowed a question?' Jack asked, and Melville nodded. 'Pardon what may be my naivety, but if our Prince Albert is the uncle of the Kaiser, why is his nephew seemingly out to prevent him from claiming his birthright?'

Melville gave a hollow laugh. 'The two hate each other, and have done for years. It seemingly stems from Wilhelm's treatment of his mother, Victoria, the firstborn and eldest daughter of the late queen, and of course the older sister of Prince Albert. Wilhelm's was a difficult birth that left him with a withered arm, for which he always blamed his mother. When his father died, he had the royal palace surrounded by troops, as though suspecting his mother of involvement in his father's death, given his appalling record for adultery. Albert was incensed by this treatment of his sister, describing it in a letter to her as "simply revolting". Wilhelm somehow learned of the letter, and the two men thereafter walked around each other like two prize fighters about to engage. In fact, there's a credible account of one occasion — following the annual yacht race at Cowes between the two, which Albert had lost — when Albert struck Wilhelm on the mouth, knocking him to the ground, after Wilhelm began mocking his loss.'

'So the two are enemies?' Percy asked.

'That's right,' Melville confirmed. 'To the extent that we are convinced, in Special Branch, that Wilhelm is anxious to prevent Albert from attaining the throne. This is clearly an unacceptable interference with our own monarchy.'

'These family history lessons are all very well,' Bruce intervened grumpily, 'but I'm only too aware of the time constraints. My watch tells me that the lunch hour is upon us, and I propose to take Superintendent Melville into the senior officers' dining room as my guest. Ordinarily, of course, I could be accompanied by Chief Inspector Enright as well, and at a push you could come along as a special civilian guest, Percy, but in the circumstances we're a little reluctant to make a public display of our current liaison with you.'

'You mean you don't want to be seen in such bad company, don't you?' Percy retorted. 'But have no fear, since Chief

Inspector Enright and myself have our own little select luncheon establishment. What time do you wish to reconvene?'

'Does that mean that you're prepared to take on this delicate assignment?' Bruce asked hopefully.

Percy rose to his feet. 'We'll give you our answer after we've partaken of a splendid lunch that I'd wager will far exceed yours in quality, although not in the price to be paid for it by the taxpaying public. Shall we say two o'clock?'

CHAPTER THREE

'So tell me what you regard as the most significant fact we've been given so far regarding this allegation of a double murder by Prince Albert,' Percy challenged Jack as they sat perusing the menu at their favourite lunch establishment, Tang Li's Chophouse on the Embankment.

'No idea,' Jack replied absentmindedly as he tried to choose between meat pie and chicken chow mien, 'and we haven't agreed to take the case on yet, although why Bruce wants to include me on the team escapes me.'

'That's obvious,' Percy replied. 'I'm not a serving officer anymore, and if we're to go blundering in after the pathetic job done by the local bobbies then he needs someone of rank to at least appear to be in charge. I'll no doubt be required to pass myself off as your manservant. Anyway, before the waiter comes to take your order, try to answer my question.'

'Remind me again?' Jack requested.

Percy sighed. 'It's probably all to the good that *if* I accept this latest commission that *you'll* get the credit for, you'll have me alongside you to focus your brain. The question was what you regard as the most significant thing we were told about what was discovered in Prince Albert's boudoir when they burst in.'

'If I sit here looking stupid for long enough, you'll tell me anyway,' Jack replied as he waved the waiter over. Their orders were quickly taken.

'How many shots were heard coming from the bedroom before the others raced up there?' prompted Percy.

'Two, according to Melville,' Jack replied confidently.

'And how many empty chambers were there in Albert's revolver?'

'Two, surely?' Jack suggested, less certain of this reply.

'No — you obviously weren't listening,' Percy admonished. 'Either that or Melville got it wrong. He actually said "three", which raises a *very* interesting question, does it not?'

'What happened to the third bullet?' Jack ventured.

'Little wonder that you made it to Chief Inspector, with deductive powers of that quality.'

'So what's your theory?'

'I don't have one, and I'm not even going to look for one until we're officially on the case.'

'If we are, we'll have to travel to this place in — where was it again?'

'Somewhere in Buckinghamshire,' Percy supplied. 'How far's that from Watford?'

'Not a clue,' Jack admitted, 'but it has to be closer to Watford than it is to Whitehall, so you no doubt have in mind staying with us while you investigate, assuming that you take the job?'

'No, Jack, while *we* investigate. And we might even employ that sharp brain of Esther's to draw conclusions from the clues that we unearth.'

'So we're going it take it on?'

'I've got nothing better lined up at present,' Percy admitted, 'while you, I imagine, would welcome a break from all those recruitment interviews. So yes, why not?'

'It could take well over a week,' Jack pointed out.

'More like a month, I suspect, which will not go down well with your aunt, given that I'll be residing with you and your family, if I take your earlier remark as an implied invitation.'

'Esther still hasn't quite forgiven you for that adverse publicity for the school after you spoke to the newspapers.'

'But she was pleased enough with the second interview I gave them, after we uncovered the plot to ruin the school and rescued young Annabelle from the circus. How is she faring as part of the Enright family, by the way?'

'She's settled in very happily, and is now a much more outgoing girl than she was while under the influence of that dreadful stepfather,' Jack replied. 'And she's progressing well in her studies, thanks to your generosity in paying her fees until she reaches twelve years of age.'

'That's set me thinking,' Percy announced, just as the waiter laid the plate of meat pie and vegetables down in front of him, 'but I'll leave my thoughts to marinate while I investigate the curative properties of this meat pie in removing the memory of those bacon and eggs that your Aunt Beattie inflicted on me at breakfast. You could have used her so-called fried eggs as ordnance for siege cannons, while her bacon rashers could have been employed to cut through iron bars. No wonder you settled for a kipper.'

'A well-developed self-defence mechanism,' Jack said with a grin as his chow mien was laid down in front of him. 'Experimental outcomes have demonstrated that even an overdone kipper in white sauce can rest more easily in the human stomach than anything fried to death. So let's eat, then you can tell me what thoughts entered your brain at the mention of Annabelle.'

Ten minutes later, both men pushed their empty plates away, and Percy picked up where they'd left off.

'Beattie was very touched when I told her that I'd waved any fee due from Emily Allsop for my unmasking the man who had a vendetta against her, and invested it in the education of a girl of eight. Her only quibble was that I hadn't brought the girl home with me. As you know, we're childless — which, incidentally, is something else your aunt blames me for — and she's always craved the experience of being a mother. She's forever asking to meet the girl again, so I thought that while we journey into Buckinghamshire on a daily basis, resting our weary heads in Watford each night, Beattie might be invited to await us there, getting to know Annabelle and playing the "extra aunt" role.'

'That sounds like an excellent arrangement,' Jack replied, 'provided that Esther doesn't let her near the kitchen. Fortunately we have Polly to do the cooking, and won't require Aunt Beattie to do any *over*cooking. Now, let's go and enquire what arrangements Melville is proposing to enable us to prevent the English throne going to someone other than Prince Albert.'

'I don't imagine that we had any choice, after what you shared with us this morning,' Percy announced as he and Jack sat back in front of Bruce's desk, with a clearly nervous Superintendent Melville seated between them. 'If we decline now, you'd no doubt arrange for us to fall victim to unfortunate accidents, so we accept.'

'What he said,' Jack murmured in confirmation, and while Melville sat back with a sigh of relief, Bruce went into organisational mode.

'As you'll both be aware,' he began, 'Scotland Yard is occasionally called in to investigate matters that have arisen under the jurisdiction of outlying police forces that are inadequately equipped to deal with them, or because they are of national importance. The matter brought to your attention this morning clearly falls into the latter category, and the Home

Secretary has already alerted the Buckinghamshire Constabulary that the Yard will be sending officers out there to take over what they probably regard as a "closed case". You'll be treading on sensitive toes, remember, and I'll be relying on Jack to play the diplomacy card, and stop Percy getting up the wrong noses. That will be particularly true when you interview Prince Albert, as I imagine you will need to do in due course. He's installed in Buckingham Palace now, and intent on becoming Edward the Seventh. Any questions thus far, apart from the size of Percy's fee?'

'Will I be going in at my current rank?' Jack asked.

'Yes, since there are no other chief inspectors even here inside the Yard, and you'll outrank everyone in Buckinghamshire except its chief constable. Percy will go with you, posing as your sergeant, although we imagine that most of the actual investigating will be done by him.'

'What about my existing duties?' Jack asked.

'Today is Tuesday, and sometime this morning Her late Majesty will be lowered into her sarcophagus inside the mausoleum at Frogmore,' Bruce told him. 'The extra men you allocated to supplement our Windsor station can return to wherever you got them from, which was presumably A Division. I can ensure that this occurs, which leaves you free of all those extra burdens you took on for the funeral. I'm sure that Sergeant Blackwell can cover the routine recruitment interviews, and I'll allocate someone of appropriate rank to do the difficult ones. That leaves you free to officially take over the Bradenham matter.'

'Beg pardon, sir?'

Melville tutted. 'Bradenham House is where the double deaths occurred. Note my choice of words, Chief Inspector —

"deaths", not "murders". There is to be no suggestion that someone has accused Prince Albert of murder, understood?'

'Since the idea never seems to have occurred to the local ninnies, why would we mention it?' Percy asked.

'I hope that you at least *appear* more respectful of the local force when you meet up with them, which I suggest should be your first action,' Melville said disapprovingly.

'About that, sir,' Jack said as he looked across the desk at Bruce, 'I had rather hoped to take a couple of days off, in lieu of the weekend I gave up for the funeral, and Uncle Percy and I have decided to use my place in Watford as our home base. Will it be in order for us to begin our enquiries on, say, Friday of this week?'

'I suppose so,' Bruce replied reluctantly after seeking a confirmatory nod from Melville, 'but no later than that, understood? I'm allocating a coach and driver to you, name of Jennings — the coachman, that is. Do you have room at your place, or will we need to accommodate him in a local hotel, assuming that Watford has one?'

'You will, sir, and it does,' Jack told him. 'Appropriately, it's called the Horse and Groom.'

'Very well. I think that just about wraps things up for this morning,' said Bruce, 'unless you have anything else, William?'

'Enright's fee?' Melville growled.

Percy appeared to think carefully before replying, 'This case is unique, as I mentioned earlier, so my fee will be commensurate with that.'

'I don't care what bloody fee you hit us with,' said Melville. 'Just pull Prince Albert out of trouble!'

Once she had recovered from the surprise of seeing her husband and nephew returning home earlier than usual, in a police coach complete with driver, Beattie Enright was delighted to be told that the following day, Wednesday, she would be travelling with them to Watford. There she would meet the girl whose school fees Percy had taken care of, and spend as much time with Esther and her family as she could while Percy and Jack conducted seemingly clandestine enquiries in Buckinghamshire.

'I shall, of course, have to advise the vicar that he'll be without my services for a while,' she said. 'Is there a suitable Methodist church in Watford that I can attend on Sundays?'

'I'm sure there are several,' Jack replied, unsure whether or not this was the case, 'and on Thursday I've promised to take Lily and Annabelle to a fair that's being held in the park behind our house. You can come with us, and get to know Annabelle a little better.'

'Can the girl read yet?' Beattie asked.

'She does little else. While Lily's intent on sewing, Annabelle sits alongside her and reads one book after another from that small library at her school.'

'Excellent!' Beattie replied. 'I have quite a collection of my own that I've acquired over the years, in the diminishing hope that I'd have a child of my own to share them with. I feel sure that the girl would appreciate those entrancing *Alice* books by the wonderfully talented Mr Carroll…'

'We'll be departing at around nine tomorrow morning,' Percy told her brusquely, before she embarked on an entire catalogue of popular children's books, 'so we'll need an early breakfast.'

'That will be no problem, if you'll settle for porridge and toast,' she told him. 'And for dinner this evening there's a pork roast, so we can make sandwiches from the leftovers for a picnic on our journey, assuming that there's any left over from this evening.'

'I'm sure there will be,' Percy muttered ominously, 'but now you might want to think about packing some clothes.'

A little after midday the following day, they arrived at the Enright house in Watford. Alice came to the front door when she heard the coach crunching through the gravel on the front drive, and smiled when she recognised its occupants. Jennings took the coach on into Watford, with instructions to return at nine on the Friday morning, and Jack, Percy and Beattie accepted Alice's offer to see what the cook, Polly, could rustle up for lunch.

Shortly before four o'clock Esther returned from the school with Lily and Annabelle, who smiled politely and bowed her head almost in reverence as she was introduced to Beattie. 'What am I to call you?' she asked.

"Aunt Beattie's" been good enough for Jack over the years, and Lily and the others got into the habit of calling me the same, because "Great Aunt Beattie" makes me sound like an ancient fossil.'

Bertie was home from his Board school not long afterwards. He was delighted to advise his great aunt that he'd become a new recruit in the Boys' Battalion being assembled by the Earl of Essex.

Beattie looked sideways at Jack as she enquired, 'Did you give your approval for that?'

'Apparently,' Jack replied. 'But ask Esther, since on her head be it if he breaks a leg or something.'

The remaining children, Miriam and Tommy, were easily won over by the bags of sweets that Beattie had acquired from a shop in Edgware, where she'd insisted they stop off during their journey north.

The following day, Thursday, Jack kept his promise to take the two older girls to the local fair, accompanied by Aunt

Beattie. The trip was a great success, and Annabelle and Beattie developed a swift rapport as they talked about the books that Beattie had brought with her. Late on the Thursday afternoon, while the two of them were in a huddle in front of the sitting room fire and the remaining children indulged in their usual activities under her supervision, Esther invited Jack and Percy to join her in the dining room for pre-dinner drinks.

'This would be a convenient time for the two of you to explain what you're up to,' she announced as she handed Percy his whisky and soda and poured two glasses of sherry for herself and Jack.

Percy chuckled. 'Ever the perceptive Esther, and as it transpires we may well have need of that acute brain of yours once we begin our investigations in darkest Buckinghamshire.'

'Dispense with the oil, Percy,' she replied with a smile. 'Jack's duties normally keep him in London, and you're no longer a serving police officer. One does not need the wisdom of Solomon to deduce that this is something out of the ordinary, so what is it? And please don't say that you're sworn to secrecy — at least, not if you want me to contribute in due course.'

'I can give you only the barest outline,' Percy told her. 'We've been sent to investigate an alleged double murder on a country estate in Buckinghamshire. It seems that the local force bungled their initial enquiries, and mistook the incident for a tragic accident. Our task is to deduce what actually happened, and it would be ideal if we can return here regularly and report the facts as we unearth them. We can then benefit from your fresh eyes, as it were.'

'And why have they called you back in, when you're supposed to have retired?'

'My proven skills as an investigator, clearly,' Percy replied smoothly.

'And Jack?'

'He's my cover. The matter has officially become one for the Yard, and Jack's the one being sent by Superintendent Melville as the official Yard person.'

'Melville?' Esther echoed. 'Wasn't he the one who damned near got Jack killed during an assassination attempt on the queen during her jubilee dinner, and talked my brother Abe into kidnapping me for my own safety?'

'The very same,' Percy confirmed with a grin.

'Then this is clearly *far* from being a routine matter,' Esther said with a frown. 'What have you two idiots got yourself into this time?'

'We'll let you know when *we* know,' Percy assured her as he held out his glass for a refill.

CHAPTER FOUR

'This seems to be taking forever,' Jack complained as their coach rattled and swayed through Beaconsfield on its journey from Watford to the far side of Buckinghamshire in the middle of Friday morning. 'How long before we reach Bradenham House?'

'Tomorrow, probably,' Percy replied. 'I suspect that the whole of today will be taken up in a long conversation with Inspector Darrow. If you recall what Melville told us, he's the inspector who was called to Bradenham immediately after the two deaths. And remember also that you have to call me Sergeant Percival, and advise anyone who needs to know that I'll be the one conducting the enquiry at ground level.'

'If it's going to take over two hours in each direction every day,' Jack grumbled, 'then we might have to rethink our original plan to return to Watford every evening.'

'We weren't given any budget for staying at local hotels,' Percy reminded him.

An hour later, they were installed in front of Inspector Darrow's desk in the narrow confines of High Wycombe Police Station, and he was eyeing them warily.

'Why does Scotland Yard think that the matter needs to be reinvestigated?' he asked with obvious suspicion. 'It was signed off by the chief constable as a double death resulting from a duel.'

'I have several queries to raise, if I may,' Percy replied. 'First of all, why did it need your chief to sign off on it, when you were the senior officer in charge of the investigation?'

'Protocol, largely,' Darrow replied blandly, 'in view of the identity of one of those who had witnessed it. If the matter had remained as an open enquiry, that person might have been required as a witness, which would not have been seemly even at the time, and now that he's about to become our king…'

His explanation tailed off as he caught the expression on Percy's face, and Percy allowed the silence to lengthen before he spoke again. 'We are all reminded, when we take the oath of office as police officers, that the law applies equally to all persons, regardless of rank or station in life,' he said. 'Or are there special rules here in Buckinghamshire?'

'Obviously not,' Darrow replied uncomfortably as he dropped his gaze to his desk, 'but I was also told when I joined the force that I was to obey orders from senior officers. If the chief constable was of the opinion that the deaths were the result of a duel, then it was not my place to contradict him.'

'Even though certain facts sit awkwardly with that verdict?' Percy prodded.

Darrow looked for assistance at Jack, who had thus far remained silent following the opening introductions. 'Which of you is conducting this review?' he asked.

'Both of us,' Jack insisted, 'and it's not a "review", it's a fresh enquiry.'

'You mean that someone has doubts about it being a duelling matter?' Darrow asked.

'Yes — just as you do, if you'd be frank enough to admit it,' Percy replied curtly. 'And don't give us any more nonsense about being overruled by a senior officer — how could *anyone* with half a brain have concluded that the two men killed each other? Did your chief constable even attend the scene?'

'No,' Darrow admitted. 'He based his conclusions on the report I'd submitted.'

'A written report?' Percy asked.

Darrow shook his head. 'No, only what I'd witnessed when I attended.'

'And how closely did you examine that bedchamber?'

'In what way?' Darrow asked.

'*Properly*!' Percy all but yelled. 'With an eye to certain obvious uncomfortable facts.'

'Such as?'

'Well, we'll start with the number of firearms in the room,' Percy suggested.

'Only one — the one on the bedside table.'

'The Webley belonging to Prince Albert — the one with three empty chambers out of the five?' Percy asked.

'Yes, that one.'

'Then where was the second one?'

'There *wasn't* a second one — I already told you that,' said Darrow, starting to sound exasperated.

'I'm finding it hard to understand how two people on either side of a room could kill each other at the same time with only one revolver,' Percy said caustically. 'Let's call them "A" and "B", shall we, for the purpose of conducting the most elementary of analyses? A fires a fatal shot at B, who, prior to dying, succeeds in wrestling the gun from B, then shooting him dead. And somewhere in that unlikely sequence of events, one of them takes the time to put the fatal weapon down on the bedside table before walking — or was it staggering? — back to where his body was found. Have I missed something?'

'Nothing that occurs to me,' Darrow admitted.

'And the little matter of the extra shot that had been fired from the revolver?' Percy demanded. When Darrow stared back at him blankly, Percy went on, 'Those who had been present downstairs during this already implausible incident reported only hearing two shots, correct?'

'That's what they reported, yes,' Darrow conceded.

'But there were three empty chambers in the magazine of the weapon you say caused the two deaths?'

'We had that confirmed by an experienced firearms specialist,' Darrow insisted, clearly considering himself on firmer ground. 'The two bullets found in the two corpses had definitely been fired from the same weapon — the one on the bedside table.'

'And where was the third bullet?'

'We didn't know if one had been fired at that time, and from all the available evidence it seemed that the third bullet must have been fired at some time earlier than the fatal shots.'

'So, of course, during the course of your "thorough" investigation, you searched for a third bullet?'

'We never found one,' Darrow told him.

Percy snorted. 'That doesn't quite answer the question I asked, but let's move on, shall we? Did the police doctor confirm that both victims had died at approximately the same time?'

This time Darrow's face turned pale as he all but whispered, 'We didn't call any doctor. Both men were obviously dead.'

'I sincerely hope that someone calls a medical expert to certify "life extinct" if I'm ever found in suspicious circumstances,' Percy muttered, 'since premature burial doesn't appeal to me in the slightest. But moving on, you presumably examined the weapon that had obviously fired the fatal shots for finger impressions?'

'Of course, and there weren't any. We assumed that the person responsible had been wearing gloves.'

'And the royal personage present in the bedchamber, with the weapon on his side table, was *he* wearing gloves?'

'No.'

'So you thought it safe to conclude that his hadn't been the hand on the weapon?'

'Naturally. That's why we concluded that the two dead men must have shot each other.'

'Were either of them wearing gloves?'

'Not that I recall.'

'Yes or no, Inspector?'

'No.'

'So did it not strike you as strange that *two* men had succeeded in grasping that weapon in turn, neither of them wearing gloves, without leaving finger impressions?'

'No, not really,' Darrow replied weakly, clearly under a great deal of stress.

'Arising from all of this, did it not occur to you as at least a possibility that a third party might have fired both shots?'

'There was no-one else in the room.'

'Not by the time you arrived, certainly,' Percy pointed out. 'But were the witnesses asked if anyone else had been in the room when they raced in to find the two men dead?'

'Not by me, certainly.'

'By any of your men?'

'Not that they reported, no.'

'Was there any other way in and out of that room, other than by means of the door from the corridor?'

'There was an adjoining dressing room-cum-bathroom, but the door to it was locked on the inside. The bedchamber side, I mean.'

'Again, it was locked by the time that you arrived, but I don't suppose that anyone in your team thought to ask if it had been locked when the others burst into the bedchamber?'

'Again, no such matter was reported.'

Percy looked sideways at Jack, and asked, 'Do you have any questions of your own, sir?'

Jack kept a straight face as he replied, 'No, Sergeant, you would seem to have asked all the relevant ones.'

'I have many more to ask,' Percy insisted, 'but I think that will be enough for one day. Before asking more questions of Inspector Darrow to which he has no credible answers, I think we need to take a look at the scene of this incident for ourselves. We'll probably be back sometime next week, Inspector.'

'What did you make of that?' Jack asked as the coach headed back towards Watford.

Percy shook his head. 'Inspector Darrow is clearly a very loyal man,' he replied.

'Loyal to Prince Albert, you mean?'

'No, loyal to his chief constable, who is most likely the one loyal to Prince Albert. But even at this early stage that loyalty would seem to have been unnecessary, since my instinct tells me that there was another person in there, apart from those who've already been identified. And Prince Albert probably wouldn't have had enough time to wipe his finger impressions off the handle of the revolver before the other members of the party raced in.'

'And wasn't he wearing a blindfold?' Jack reminded him.

'Was he?' Percy replied. 'We didn't get round to that little matter, since I considered that we'd rattled Darrow's cage hard enough. I'd be prepared to wager that when we return next week, his loyalty to his chief constable will have become somewhat diluted.'

'But before that you intend to visit the scene of the crime?'

'Most definitely. I hope also to interview the widow while we're there, assuming that she's still in residence. And, as an added bonus, a butler, footman or someone whose loyalty to his former master and current mistress doesn't extend to lying as fervently as Inspector Darrow.'

'So what do you propose that we do over the weekend?' Jack asked.

Percy sat back in the coach with a contented smile. 'Whatever you normally do at the weekend. One thing I suggest we do, however, is test my hypothesis on Esther. A third opinion would be most valuable at this stage.'

'A *third* opinion?'

'Yes. The second is yours.'

'I don't have one at present, I'm afraid — other than the fact that Inspector Darrow's covering something up, or perhaps seeking to minimise his own incompetence.'

'No-one could be that incompetent, Jack, not if he's experienced enough to have made it to Inspector rank. He's clearly been bought — or overawed — into silence. The real question is, by whom? Hence our need to travel to Bradenham on Monday, after what hopefully will prove to be a restful weekend.'

Esther and the children were delighted to learn that Jack and Percy were taking two days off to be in their company for an entire weekend. On Saturday morning, Beattie insisted that Percy escort her on a cursory visit to two local Methodist churches identified by Esther's employer Emily Allsop. Having opted to loan her religious fervour to a local Wesleyan Mission the following day, and exempting Percy from the need to accompany her in return for his agreement that Annabelle could visit them for a few days during the Easter holidays, she and Percy returned in time for a late lunch.

On Sunday morning Beattie duly took herself off to worship, while the children sat around the fire gazing out of the window at another lazy snowfall that was converting Cassiobury Park, to the rear of the house, into a white landscape on which Lily, Annabelle and Miriam could imagine sledges and white horses pulling fairytale princesses towards their glittering palaces. Meanwhile, Bertie insisted on advising his younger brother Tommy of the difficulties of moving entire armies across snowy countryside, adding a stirring account of how the deep drifts surrounding Moscow had finally defeated Napoleon.

Percy took advantage of everyone else being thus occupied to suggest that he and Jack sit with Esther in the dining room, in which Alice already had a roaring fire going. Once they were seated, Percy, armed with a school notebook and pencil that he'd borrowed from Lily, announced, 'It's time for us to seek Esther's confirmation of a theory that I've begun to develop regarding this latest business that we're investigating.'

'So you really *do* intend to involve me, do you?' Esther smiled. 'It wasn't just idle flattery designed to wheedle yourself back into my good books?'

'I rather thought I'd already done that when I offered free schooling for young Annabelle, who I must admit has come on a treat since you took her under your wing. Quite the young lady, and Beattie was asking if it would be in order for her to spend a few days with us in Hackney during the Easter school holidays.'

'Of course,' Esther agreed, 'but let's not drift from your first point. What's your theory?'

'I don't want to risk putting any ideas into your head before you give me your candid opinion on what I'm about to reveal. I believe that a certain conclusion can be drawn from the facts I'm about to relate, with the aid of a crude diagram, and Jack can correct me if I omit any important details. So, let's begin, shall we?'

Percy drew a simple rectangle on the clean sheet of paper, added four capital letters in specific locations inside it, then passed it across to Esther. 'This is a bedroom, and the capital letters depict four people inside it at the crucial moment,' he told her. 'Person A is seated by the bed, we believe blindfolded, while B is being led into that bedroom, also believed to be blindfolded, by C. Also, located somewhere in the centre of the room, is D. Two gunshots ring out, and C and D are discovered dead, both from bullets fired from a revolver located on a table at the side of the bed. Your first question, if you have one?'

'I believe that it's possible to identify offenders by any finger impressions they've left behind, is that correct?' Esther asked.

Percy nodded. 'The technique is in its infancy, but yes, you're basically correct.'

'And were any finger impressions located on the pistol?'

'None, or so we've been informed.'

'And the person we're calling "A" — the one seated by the bed — you say that he or she was blindfolded?'

'So we're told, although I have my doubts on that point.'

'But even if they weren't, and if their finger impressions weren't on the revolver, were they wearing gloves?'

'Again, we don't know for certain, but assume that they weren't.'

'And what about that other person — B — who was being led into the room blindfolded?'

'What about them?'

'Were they wearing gloves?'

'We haven't yet ascertained that, or whether or not they really *were* blindfolded,' Percy told her, 'but B was a lady who had until that moment been relaxing after dinner with other ladies, and might well therefore have been wearing gloves.'

'Then she could have fired the two shots, then placed the gun beside A in order to incriminate them.'

'And if she *wasn't* wearing gloves?'

'Then she couldn't have fired the shots.'

'Then who did?'

'No-one that you've identified, clearly.'

'If we assume that neither C nor D were wearing gloves, then would you rule them both out as the one who fired the shots?'

'Obviously, for the same reason — the lack of finger impressions on the weapon.'

'And if they *were* both wearing gloves, could they have killed each other?'

Esther thought hard for a moment, an exasperated expression on her face, then voiced her opinion. 'Are you seriously suggesting that C first shot D, then D, while dying, somehow got the gun from C and shot him, following which one of them managed to put the gun down on the side table in order to implicate A?'

'It *has* been suggested,' Percy replied with a grin.

'But that's preposterous!' Esther objected. 'Quite ludicrous!'

'So what alternative can you suggest?'

'Is there more than one entrance to this room, other than the one through which B was being led?'

'We're advised that there's an adjoining room containing dressing and sanitary facilities, but we haven't yet visited the scene. Such information as we've been given suggests that the dividing door between the two rooms was locked.'

'Locked at the time that the bodies were discovered, but not necessarily at the time of the shooting?'

'Brilliant!' Percy couldn't help himself from declaring. 'If the dividing door *wasn't* locked at the time, what conclusion might you draw?'

'Clearly, the presence of another party,' Esther replied. 'Someone perhaps taking advantage of the fact that A and B, the only two survivors, were blindfolded, in order to fire two shots, then retreat into that side room. But how did they manage to lock it from the bedroom side?'

'You really *should* be a detective!' Percy said gleefully. 'You've reached the same conclusion as me — there was someone else present who made a hasty departure after committing the two murders while wearing gloves, then left the revolver on the side table in order to implicate A.'

It fell silent. Jack was mentally agreeing with Percy that Esther's absence from the Met, which didn't employ women, was a huge detriment to law enforcement, when she spoke again.

'You and Jack have clearly been allocated this case because someone important is involved. May I assume that this mysterious third person is someone very well known — someone sufficiently elevated in public life for Special Branch to want to protect their identity?'

'Well surmised,' Percy murmured, 'and you've got the sentiment right, although the person who's being protected is the one I depicted as A on the diagram — someone who's suspected of being the murderer. You've eliminated that person in theory, employing the same logic as me, but now we have to find the hard evidence to prove that A was being "set up", to use the vulgar expression currently being employed on the street.'

'And am I allowed to know who A is?' Esther asked.

Percy looked enquiringly at Jack, who nodded, adding, 'No harm, I suppose.'

'Very well,' Percy agreed. 'The person I called A is in fact our future king, except that someone is attempting to prevent that.'

'You mean…?' Esther began, reluctant to name the person in question.

'The very same,' Percy confirmed. 'Prince Albert Edward, heir to the throne, whose eventual coronation may have to be cancelled unless we can come up with answers to this conundrum.'

CHAPTER FIVE

Jennings had the coach outside the front door at precisely eight o'clock on the Monday morning as instructed. Percy bid him a cheery good morning as he and Jack climbed quickly into the coach to dodge the sleet shower that had suddenly begun falling.

'I trust you had a relaxing weekend?' Percy asked just before he closed the door.

'I was able to go home to Islington — thank you for enquiring,' Jennings replied. 'It wasn't snowing there, and it looks as if a thaw has set in here, so the roads should be passable. Where to this morning, sirs?'

'Bradenham House, which is the other side of High Wycombe, on the road to Aylesbury,' Percy instructed him, and he and Jack sat back in anticipation of a two-hour journey, both of them heavily wrapped against the raw conditions.

'So we're going to speak to this American widow, are we?' Jack asked.

Percy nodded. 'Her correct name is Lady Virginia Belvedere, and if she's like the other American recruits to English society that I've met, she'll be very jealous of the title and conscious of the protocols, so be obsequious. You don't actually have to touch your forelock these days, but try to look suitably grateful to be in her presence.'

'You're the socialist in the family,' Jack reminded him, 'so presumably you'll be more impressed when we interview the butler, or steward, or whoever.'

'They're bigger snobs than their employers, in my experience,' Percy muttered with obvious distaste. 'And if anyone in the house we're about to visit will be keen to minimise the sins of its owners, it'll be the resident flunkey.'

It was late morning by the time Bradenham House came into view at the end of its long, straight drive. It was sturdily built from red brick and had three storeys, the topmost, with its narrower dormer windows, betraying the fact that it was constructed with live-in servants in mind. There was a man trimming a large azalea bush on the final approach to the front door, and as Percy and Jack descended from the coach, Jack displayed his police badge and asked who they might speak to regarding the recent event that had left the former master of the house dead.

'That'll be Davenport,' the man replied. 'Mester Davenport's the steward, and you'll find him in the 'ouse. Just ring that there bell at the door.'

They did as instructed, and the sound that seemed to fill the entire front hall beyond the partly opened front doors reminded Jack of cathedral bells. In due course a tall, elderly man appeared and opened the doors fully as he looked down his aquiline nose at the pair of them.

'Yes, what brings you here?' he asked suspiciously. 'Her Ladyship is not at home to callers, and we were not expecting any visitors.'

'We're the sort of visitors who no-one expects,' Percy replied coldly, and Jack held up his police badge before the man they assumed to be the steward took them for burglars caught in the act.

The man squinted hard at the badge, then asked, 'Is it about the recent incident? The police investigated that fully at the time.'

'That's debateable,' Percy argued, 'and in view of the high-profile person who was involved in it, Scotland Yard obviously has an interest in tying up any loose ends.'

'If you say so,' the man conceded grudgingly. 'I'm Claude Davenport, and I have the privilege of being the steward to the Belvedere estate. I suppose you'd like to see where the unfortunate business occurred?'

'If we may,' Jack replied, before Percy could say anything sarcastic.

Davenport led them solemnly up a flight of ornate stairs, on which two maids in service smocks were busily engaged in sweeping the carpet. They were on their knees with dustpans and brushes, and visibly increased the pace of their brushing when they became aware of Davenport's approach.

At the head of the stairs Davenport turned left, then led them past a door on the right-hand side until they reached a second door, which he pushed open with a gloved hand.

'This is it, gentlemen,' he announced. 'It hasn't been touched since — well, since that evening, as it happens. That was some months ago now, of course, and I will not be answerable for the state of it.'

'Who gave the instruction for it to remain untouched?' Percy asked.

Davenport gave a disapproving twitch of his nose as he replied, 'The local police inspector — a somewhat earthy man with very little sense of occasion. We were very honoured to have Prince Albert as our guest that evening, and it was doubly unfortunate that events occurred as they did.'

'Why do you say "doubly" unfortunate?' Percy asked.

Davenport pulled a long face as he replied, 'We lost the master that night, as the result of an ill-advised duel. One would have thought that those unseemly behaviours from a bygone age were no longer in vogue, but then I have long since ceased to be surprised by anything that modern persons of quality engage in.'

'And the second misfortune?' Percy prompted him.

'The fact that it occurred in front of our royal guest, obviously. He hasn't been back here since, and of course he then had the misfortune of the death of his mother.'

'Quite,' Percy replied as he began to survey the bedroom. 'You say that nothing has changed since that night?'

'No,' Davenport replied with obvious distaste. 'I haven't even been allowed to instruct the cleaners to come in here, and that carpet will clearly need to be replaced.' He nodded down at an ominous dark brown stain that was only too visible against the pale green of the carpet.

'Which of them was that?' Percy asked. 'I assume that one of the bodies ended up there.'

'That would be the master, sir,' Davenport replied with what was almost a shudder. 'The other one was in the middle of the room there — Wilson, the master's valet, who'd been assigned to the prince for that weekend.'

'And absolutely nothing has changed in here?' Percy asked.

'Not since that night, no, although the prince obviously chose to reassign that bedside table.'

Percy and Jack looked at where Davenport was pointing, to a table that sat to the right of the bed as one looked across at it. The bed itself was against the far wall, with the bed-head hard up against it, and a few feet away from the bed itself was a door.

'We were told that the door over there leads to a dressing room with sanitary facilities,' Percy said. 'Is that the case?'

'Correct,' Davenport confirmed, 'and *that* hasn't even been entered since the incident, let alone cleaned.'

'You mentioned that the prince had moved the bedside table,' Jack recalled.

'Yes,' Davenport confirmed. 'It used to be to the left of the bed, but for some reason it was moved to the right-hand side, presumably on the prince's instruction. That would have been done by the valet, of course.'

'The one who died in the duel?' Percy asked.

Again Davenport nodded with obvious distaste. 'Quite why the master and his valet came to engage in a duel escapes me, although that somewhat gauche police inspector hinted that it might have been a matter impugning the honour of Her Ladyship.'

'Returning to the matter of the adjoining door to the bathroom,' Percy said, 'was it locked when people rushed in here following the sound of gunshots?'

'Yes, indeed, sir,' said Davenport, 'just as you see it now. As I said, nothing has been touched, and nobody's accessed the dressing room beyond.'

'Not even the police?' Percy asked. 'You're quite certain of that?'

'Absolutely, sir.' Davenport smiled with satisfaction. 'Once they arrived, I took it upon myself to remain in this room to ensure that nothing was damaged, or — may I say it — removed. I was most meticulous about that.'

'And that door was as we see it now, locked, and with the key inside the lock itself?'

'Yes, sir.'

'Perhaps you might tell us the *precise* course of events that evening, as you experienced them,' Jack invited him, determined that this was not about to turn into a one-man investigation.

'Of course,' Davenport agreed. 'I'd been dividing my duties between the sitting room, in which the ladies were located and were being served with coffee by the parlourmaid Ettie, and the dining room, in which the men had remained, and I was ensuring that the port and brandy didn't run out. I was actually in the sitting room when the master entered and called for the mistress to accompany him outside. I believe that they went into the morning room across the hallway from the sitting room, although I can't be certain. Then I was on my way to the wine store for more port when I noticed the master and mistress mounting the main staircase. I though it a little unusual for them to be retiring for the night in the circumstances, and then just as I'd placed the extra port bottle on the hall stand, ahead of uncorking it and taking it into the dining room, I heard what sounded like two gunshots. Not shotguns, such as they'd been using during the day, but more like the reports from a pistol. The men in the dining room must have heard them too, along with the ladies in the sitting room, because several of them — ladies *and* gentlemen — raced out of the two rooms and asked me where the gunshot sounds had come from. I indicated that it sounded like the bedroom allocated to the prince, and I followed behind when they raced up to see what had happened. The door was still open, and we could all clearly see the scene before us.'

'You all clearly witnessed what *appeared* to have happened,' Percy corrected him. 'You're quite certain in your own mind that there were only two shots fired?'

'I think I can be relied upon to count to two, sir,' Davenport replied frostily.

'Tell us *exactly* the scene that met your eyes when you got into this room,' Percy insisted.

Davenport appeared to be reliving the event as he half-closed his eyes. 'The master was lying on the carpet just inside the door — in fact, we needed to step over his body in order to access the room proper. Her Ladyship was just inside the room, screaming hysterically, and the prince was seated on the side of the bed — the right-hand side as you look towards it, with the bedside table slightly behind him. There was a weapon on the side table, and it was only then that I noticed the second body — Wilson, as I said, who'd been in attendance on the Prince ever since his arrival. He also appeared to be dead, although in his case there wasn't as much blood as there was on the master's body. As you can see, the bloodstain left by the master was such that in due course, and when permitted by the police, we'll need to replace the carpet, but there was no such stain on Wilson — just an obvious hole through his waistcoat that was smeared a sort of brown colour.'

Percy looked meaningfully across at Jack, for reasons that escaped him. Since Davenport seemed to have concluded his narrative, Percy asked him another question.

'Do you recall if either your mistress or the prince were wearing blindfolds?'

'Neither of them at that time, sir, although there was a blindfold lying on the carpet at the prince's feet, while Her Ladyship was gripping one in her hand. As I already mentioned, she was highly distraught, and was shortly thereafter led away by several of the other ladies who'd accompanied us up there.'

'Thank you most sincerely for such a comprehensive account,' Jack said to Davenport, certain that it would not occur to Percy to do so.

Davenport preened slightly. 'In my profession, one is required to be observant, sir. Will there be anything else? Only I have my duties to attend to.'

'No, you can go,' Percy told him, in the manner of a schoolmaster dismissing an errant pupil after a chastisement, 'but we need to look more closely at this room, if you can trust us not to steal the light fittings.'

Davenport gave him a reproving stare, then bowed slightly to both men and took himself off down the hallway.

Jack looked hard at Percy. 'The man was doing his best, and you treated him almost like a suspect,' he said reproachfully.

'At present, he still is,' Percy grunted, 'since whatever went on in here cannot have been pulled off without some sort of inside assistance. The only one left to point the finger at is Davenport, since the former Belvedere valet ended up as one of the corpses.'

'So what do you propose that we do now?' Jack asked.

Percy nodded towards the door that allegedly led to the dressing room and bathroom. 'You and I are about to conduct a little experiment, if that's the sort of door I think it is, of which Davenport failed to fully advise us.'

'What do you mean?' Jack asked.

Percy smiled. 'You obviously lack the sort of experience of hotel rooms that I've recently acquired in my second career. Watch.' He led Jack to the door and turned the knob. 'Locked, yes?' he asked.

'Obviously,' Jack replied, with some petulance.

Percy then turned the key and invited Jack to try to open it. With a look of surprised annoyance, Jack turned the knob and discovered that the door would still not open when he pushed it. He tried pulling, but to no avail.

'It's clearly locked from the other side,' said Percy. 'It's what they call a "double lock" system, and it's frequently employed in hotels that have adjoining rooms.'

Jack still looked a little uncertain, so Percy gave him the benefit of a fuller explanation. 'A couple intent on a little indiscretion book into an hotel and ask for adjoining rooms. There are locks on *both* sides of the adjoining door, designed to ensure — in the event that the adjoining occupants are strangers to each other — that neither can access the room occupied by the other. But of course, to a couple whose motivation for asking for such rooms is to engage in a little "blanket hornpipe", as some navy types call it, a double access door is ideal. They can swear on a stack of bibles that the communicating door remained locked, while engaging in their liaison.'

'Yes, thank you, I get the picture,' Jack replied with a look of mild distaste. 'But if it's locked from the other side, how do we gain access to it?'

'From outside, in the reverse direction from which it was probably employed on the evening in question,' Percy replied. 'For that, we'll need to conduct a careful perusal of the layout of the first floor of this place, and then acquire the use of a stepladder.'

They moved back to the head of the staircase, and Percy observed, 'Assuming that this is the centre of the building, then counting down the hallway we've just travelled along, the bedchamber would be the second from the centre, on the north-facing wall. The bedroom itself had no external window, you'll recall, but the adjoining dressing room almost certainly does, so that's the one we're after. Follow me.'

'Where are we going?' Jack asked testily as he scuttled along behind Percy across the frost-encrusted lawn, then round to the back of the house.

Percy made no reply as he strode to the centre of the north-facing wall of the building, then counted, with his outstretched finger, two windows to the right of the centre. He gave a satisfied grunt. 'There it is!' he announced. 'Just as I predicted.'

'How do you know it's the right window?' Jack asked.

Percy gave him a sympathetic look. 'It's a good job you never thought of entering the building trade. What do you see running down to the left of that window?'

'A drainpipe, why?'

'And what sort of room comes equipped with a drainpipe?'

'Ah, yes, of course,' Jack replied, feeling slightly foolish. 'A bathroom.'

'Now, your second question of the day regarding the homes of the wealthy,' Percy said with a grin. 'What would be your first port of call within such a house for all the gossip, and general intelligence regarding what goes on?'

'In our house it would be the kitchen,' Jack replied.

Percy nodded. 'Time for a temporary change in career, Jack my boy. We're about to become locksmiths, or builders, if you prefer. And we might even qualify for something to eat, since the rumble I'm experiencing just below my pocket watch is unlikely to be coming from anywhere other than my neglected stomach.'

They walked back the way they had come until they found the scullery entrance, through which the local butcher had just made a delivery. Percy led the way through it into the kitchen, where there was a limited amount of activity taking place, and a middle-aged lady sat despondently at the centre table, dragging what looked like slices of fish through a mixture of breadcrumbs and flour soaked in milk. There was a strong smell of soup and fresh bread lingering in the air. Percy nodded appreciatively at the bowl in the hands of the lady they took to be the cook as he asked, 'Who are the lucky people who're going to be feasting on that fried fish, and will you be serving it with fried potato chippings?'

'Nobody apart from the staff, unfortunately,' the lady replied with a grimace. 'The mistress stopped eating normal meals after the master died. I'm sick and tired of just serving up fruit and cheese, so I'm doing this just so that I don't forget how to do it, and to feed the staff when they've done their morning's work.'

'More's the pity that we don't work here permanently,' Percy replied. He indicated Jack to one side of him and added, 'The boy and I are just here to fix a loose window frame around the back of the house, and I was wondering if you could tell us where we might find a stepladder, since the boneheaded boy forgot to load ours onto the wagon.'

'If you go round to the gardener's shed on the other side of the rose garden, he should have one,' the cook replied, 'and then if you'd care to come back in here after you've finished the job, I'd be delighted to let you sample my fried fish.'

Five minutes later, Jack and Percy were lining up the gardener's stepladder against the window frame. 'Thank God you never decided on a career as a fraudster,' Jack chuckled.

Percy went up the ladder first while Jack held the bottom steady. 'Just as I thought!' Percy called back down. 'It was left unlocked after someone used it as an escape route. Hang on a second while I open it fully, then follow me up here.'

Once they were both inside the dressing room, Percy pointed to a brown stain on the linoleum. 'Do you recall what

Davenport said about the second body — the one belonging to the valet?'

'Not really,' Jack admitted, 'except that it was in the centre of the room next door.'

'He said that it didn't leave a bloodstain on the carpet, like Belvedere's body had done. That's probably because the valet was done to death in here, at a guess, a good while before Belvedere was shot. *Why* the valet was shot is another question altogether, of course, unless he'd cottoned on to what was about to occur. Anyway, let's prove the accuracy of my theory about the locked door, shall we?'

Percy walked to the lock on the inside of the door, identical in appearance to the one on its other side, and first of all turned the key, then turned the knob. The door opened easily, to reveal the inside of the bedchamber they'd been in earlier. Then he turned back to Jack and stated what, to him at least, was the obvious conclusion.

'Somebody hid in here after the deed was done, safe in the knowledge that no-one could come in because the door was locked on this side. The police assumed, of course, that it was locked on the bedroom side and wasted all that time trying to puzzle out how someone other than Prince Bertie could have killed the two victims unless they'd killed each other. Since the first conclusion was unthinkable — to the chief constable, anyway — they opted for the second, ludicrous though it is.'

'Assuming that the person who locked themself in here didn't have access to a stepladder, are we to assume that they remained in here until it was safe to go out through the bedroom?' Jack asked.

Percy snorted derisively. 'I doubt if this bedroom was empty again for at least twenty-four hours after the discovery of the bodies. My guess is that they left via the same route that we came in, making use of that very handy drainpipe, and perhaps jumping down for the last few feet. The entire drop can't be more than twelve feet, and I've seen many a burglar perform that sort of feat, as no doubt have you.'

'So can we now go and claim that free lunch that you flattered the cook into producing?' Jack asked.

'Almost,' Percy replied. 'But we have one more puzzle to solve, while we're back here where it all happened. Can you deduce what it might be?'

'You know I can't, so take that smirk off your face and tell me,' Jack said grumpily.

'The little matter of the two shots that were heard by the witnesses, the probability that only one victim was shot in the presence of the blindfolded prince and Lady Belvedere, and the missing third bullet from the prince's revolver. We might have to return, perhaps with a scientific team.'

'Is there the remotest possibility that you're about to tell me why we need a scientific team?' Jack demanded.

Percy nodded first up at the ceiling, then down at the carpet, and finally along the two side walls. 'I believe that a concentrated and minute search will reveal the existence of a bullet hole somewhere in this room, perhaps even the bullet itself. If we assume for the moment that Wilson the valet was already dead, and that Belvedere got the second bullet — the first of those that the witnesses heard — the question then arises as to when, and at what, the third bullet was discharged.'

'I can't think about this on an empty stomach,' Jack said with a sigh. 'Shouldn't we be going down to claim our lunch? And, for the record, I resent being passed off as a brainless lad who forgot to load a stepladder onto a builder's cart.'

Just then, Davenport appeared in the open doorway to the hall. 'Ah, I'm glad I caught you,' he said. 'I've arranged for you to meet with her ladyship this afternoon, at, shall we say, two o'clock? It's slightly after one o'clock at present, so I've asked the cook to supply you with some lunch in the servants' hall. It's just off the kitchen.'

'Thank you,' Percy replied graciously as he gently kicked Jack's ankle to warn him to refrain from revealing that they'd already made their own arrangements with the cook. 'Where will we be meeting with Lady Virginia?'

'In the drawing room on the ground floor,' Davenport told them as he disappeared back down the hallway.

CHAPTER SIX

'Why didn't you tell us you were bobbies?' the cook demanded as Percy and Jack reappeared through the scullery door. They found the coachman, Jennings, seated at the centre table, eating bread and cheese. Clearly he had been the first one to give away Percy and Jack's true identities.

'Sorry,' he mumbled as Percy shot him a reproving stare.

'I didn't want to scare you out of providing us with some of your excellent fried fish,' said Percy, turning to the cook, 'and not everyone regards police officers as fit companions.'

'I'm told that one of you is a senior man,' the cook added, 'and that you're here in connection with what happened to the master.'

'I'm the senior man, despite appearances,' Jack told her, 'and my apologies that my underling chose to amuse himself with one of his favourite pastimes — pretending to be someone he isn't. The grey hairs come from his tortured conscience.'

'Well, now that we know who you are,' the cook sniffed, 'go and join the others in the servant's hall next door. I'll bring your meals through — not that you deserve any, trying to pull the wool over the eyes of a hardworking and honest lady like myself.'

They walked into the room indicated, where half a dozen house servants in their various uniforms sat around a table, chatting. It fell silent as Percy and Jack entered, and a young man who looked like a stable groom muttered, 'Watch what you say, ladies, else it'll go down in their bloody notebooks.'

'I'm delighted that at least one of you is familiar with police procedures,' Percy said with a smile, 'although I'll refrain from enquiring precisely how that came about.'

It fell silent again as the cook brought in their meals, with an obviously larger portion for Jack, which he switched for Percy's smaller portion once she'd returned to her kitchen. Then one of the girls announced, 'Davenport's in trouble with the mistress for not letting her know there was coppers in the place, asking how the master got shot.'

'That oversight was remedied, it would seem,' Percy said after clearing his mouth of fried fish, 'but how did she find out?'

'Davenport told the 'ousekeeper that you was here, and she musta blabbed it to the mistress,' the girl explained.

'You need to watch how you speak about Mrs Button, Ettie,' one of the other girls cautioned her. 'You know she'll 'ave you back down to chambermaid as soon as look at you.'

'"Ettie"? is that your name?' Percy asked. 'You're the parlourmaid who was serving the ladies the night that the master was shot?'

'That's me,' Ettie confirmed. 'I'm the *only* parlourmaid, because the 'ousekeeper's too mean to employ any others.'

'So what do you remember happening, just before the shootings?' Percy asked.

The stable groom muttered, 'Remember what I said about his notebook.'

'Shut your trap, Robbie Green,' Ettie fired back, clearly delighted to be at the centre of a police enquiry. She then smiled back at Percy. 'I were servin' the ladies, like you said. I was in the 'allway, ready to take in another tray of them petit fours, when the master and mistress came outta the morning room together. She was looking daggers and said something like, "I can't imagine how you could think I'd want to lie with that revolting slob." And he replied, "Well, here's your chance to prove it." Then they went upstairs, and a short time later I heard them shots, like from a gun.'

'Did you run upstairs with some of the ladies?' Percy asked.

Ettie grimaced. 'Yeah, and I wished I 'adn't when I saw Jamie lying there. The master as well, o' course, but it were Jamie what were special.'

'I told you he was no good fer you,' Robbie mumbled.

'You was just jealous, that were all!' Ettie spat back. 'Just because I preferred 'im to you!'

'So he was your suitor?' Percy coaxed her.

'Me and him 'ad this special understanding,' Ettie confirmed. 'We was meant to meet up after the midday meal earlier that day, because then the prince would be out shooting and wouldn't need 'im. Jamie were the master's valet, you see, and the master loaned him to the Prince when the other valet — the one what the prince normally uses — wanted the day off. That's what got Jamie killed, o' course, because he wouldn't't've been there otherwise. But he didn't show up for our meeting after dinner, neither.'

'So when was the last time you saw Jamie? Jamie Wilson, is that right?' Percy asked as casually as he could.

'Musta been the day afore that, when we went for a walk in the woods, except Bradley the gamekeeper chased us off in case we scared the grouse.'

'What was you doin' to scare game birds?' Robbie asked with a fruity chuckle.

'Mind your own business!' Ettie said crossly. 'Anyroad, don't think you can take over where he left off — a girl's got certain standards!'

'Time we left,' Percy muttered to Jack, and they sidled out of what was threatening to become a very unpleasant domestic dispute. Once they were outside, Percy was obviously excited.

'Amazing what people tell you without realising. What additional intelligence relating to our enquiry did you glean from that little exchange?'

'That parlourmaids regard themselves as social superiors to stable grooms?' Jack offered.

Percy laughed. 'I'll let that pass, since I've probably insulted my "senior officer" enough for one day. But I learned two things: the first is that her ladyship did indeed accept the blindfolded challenge in the prince's bedchamber because she wanted to quash any suggestion that she'd been one of his conquests. The second is that the master's valet, James Wilson — the one loaned to the prince by Belvedere — was probably dead by the middle of the day, though he officially died later that evening. That also suggests how the prince's revolver came to have three empty chambers.'

'So Wilson was shot earlier in the day?' Jack concluded. 'But how come his body ended up in the prince's bedchamber later that evening? It surely can't have been lying there for several hours in plain view?'

'*Think*, Jack,' Percy urged him with a hint of exasperation. 'We found what might be a bloodstain in that adjoining dressing room-cum-lavatory, which suggests that Wilson was shot in there. And there was a long, low chest of some sort in the dressing room, which is probably used for storing spare bed linen. It could also have been used to hide Wilson's body until the time was right to reveal it, and make it look as if the prince had shot both him *and* Belvedere at the same time. Then, in order to account for both Wilson's body *and* the missing third bullet, whoever it was discharged that third and final shot into the ceiling, or wherever.'

'But why was Wilson killed?'

'Absolutely no idea, at this stage,' Percy admitted, 'but of course we still have more interviews to conduct, beginning with her ladyship. Unless I misheard that parish clock chime as we came away from that excellent free lunch, she'll already be awaiting us in the drawing room.'

'I'm sorry I wasn't available to speak with you both earlier, but I wasn't aware that you were here,' Lady Virginia Belvedere purred in her mid-Atlantic accent as she sat across from them in her armchair. Jack and Percy were perched on the sofa, Jack admiring her cultured beauty. She was tall, slim, and had high cheekbones that accentuated her dark hazel eyes and flowing auburn locks. Jack was hoping that Percy would employ his usual flow of seemingly innocuous questions that always seemed to coax facts from witnesses without them knowing, while he, Jack, could just gaze at her entrancing face.

'We were reluctant to intrude on what will no doubt still be your understandable grief,' Percy replied unctuously, in stark contrast to the way he'd spoken to the local police inspector the previous week.

'I'm over the worst of it, I think,' Lady Virginia conceded, 'but it was quite a shock, as you can understand, seeing two people shot dead like that, one of them my husband of almost eight years.'

'So you actually *saw* what happened?' Percy probed.

'I was actually blindfolded at the time that I heard the two shots, but once I pulled off the blindfold I could see my husband lying dead on the floor, with an obvious bullet wound in his chest. I didn't know then that he was dead, of course, but that soon became pretty damned obvious.'

'I'm led to believe that no doctor was called,' Percy prompted her.

Lady Virginia shook her head. 'No. Davenport's first action, when he arrived on the scene, was to call the police, and it was the local inspector who confirmed that they were both dead.'

'The other man being your late husband's valet, James Wilson?'

'Yes, that's right. He was on loan to the prince because he'd given his man the day off in order to join the hunt earlier, and I didn't see him again that day once the shooting party came onto the rear patio for luncheon. I saw him the following morning, of course, as he accompanied the prince in his coach in order to travel back to London. I believe that he may have sustained some injury himself the previous day.'

'What sort of injury?' Percy asked as casually as he could.

'A sprained ankle or something. The ground is very uneven in the home wood where the hunt took place. Anyway, he appeared to be walking with a limp.'

'Why were you blindfolded, if I might make so bold as to enquire?' Percy asked.

Lady Virginia wrinkled her nose. 'I won't go into the sordid details, but it was a guessing game that the prince had agreed to take part in. Someone was to walk into the room, and he was to guess who it was while wearing a blindfold.'

'And how did you get to be chosen? Were there others also waiting to take part?'

'No, I was the first, and obviously, after the shootings, there could be no question of anyone else taking part.'

'So, if I understand what you were telling us,' Percy said coaxingly, 'you first of all heard the shots, then —

74

understandably, of course — you removed the blindfold. Have I got that right?'

'Yes,' Lady Virginia replied with a slight shudder. 'Forgive me, but it's not every day that you find your husband lying dead on the carpet in front of you. He'd led me into the room, you see, given that I was blindfolded. We hadn't been in there for more than a few seconds before I heard a gunshot, and sensed that Rupert — my husband — had fallen to the floor. He was slightly ahead of me, as I already said.'

'Yes, I'm getting a very good picture,' Percy assured her. 'So when did you hear the second shot? Was that before or after the shot that was presumably the one that killed Sir Rupert?'

She appeared to think carefully for a moment, then replied, 'I'm pretty sure I heard *both* shots before I pulled off my blindfold, and then once I saw what had happened to Rupert, I was oblivious to anything else. But someone behind me screamed out "Jamie", and it was then that I realised where the second shot had gone.'

'There were people behind you?'

'Yes, men and women who were our weekend guests, and a hysterical parlourmaid who was walking out with Jamie at the time. Jamie was James Wilson, my late husband's valet. An excellent man, and *very* well mannered.'

'This must seem like a strange question, Lady Virginia,' Percy said in a soft voice, 'but how tall was this Jamie?'

'A strange question indeed,' Lady Virginia replied as she looked enquiringly at Jack for confirmation that this was relevant, 'but since you ask, I'd say that he was slightly below average height. Shorter than either of you two by a good deal, and slightly built, like your buddy here.' She nodded towards Jack, who blushed slightly and looked down at the carpet. This was Percy's show, obviously, and Jack wanted to maintain her ladyship's obvious belief that he was merely there to carry the bags.

'A minor detail, if I may,' Percy said quietly, 'but were you wearing evening gloves, or gloves of any description, when you entered the room?'

'No,' Lady Virginia replied. 'I'd been wearing them earlier, but I removed them before being taken upstairs by my husband and then blindfolded when we reached the door to the bedchamber.'

'And if I might now take you back to what you saw when you first took off your blindfold,' Percy requested, 'did anything else catch your attention, other than the sight of your late husband lying on the floor?'

'Not really. It was as if I was seeing him through a narrow window, with everything around it blacked out — down a tunnel, if that helps to explain.'

'Indeed it does,' Percy assured her in a tone rich in sympathy. 'So was there anyone else in the room of whom you were aware at this time?'

'Not immediately, but eventually I saw the prince sitting on the side of the bed. My attention was really only drawn to him when I heard him call out, "What the Hell just happened?"'

'So are you aware of whether or not he saw anything for himself of what had transpired?'

'Presumably you've already spoken with him, and that's why you're here — to clear his name?'

'We have yet to speak with him, your ladyship,' Percy told her. 'But what makes you believe that his name *needs* to be cleared?'

'Well, apart from the two men who were shot, he was the only person in the room when I took off my blindfold, which gives rise to a certain inference, does it not?'

'There was absolutely no-one else?' Percy persisted.

She shook her head vigorously. 'I've obviously formed my own opinion of what happened,' she replied as her jaw line became even more pronounced and determined, 'and nothing will shake me from that. But given his position, I don't suppose he'll ever be held to account for what he did. And as for wearing a blindfold, that was clearly only a ruse. When I removed mine, he wasn't wearing one either.'

'So you've no idea whether or not he'd been wearing one when the shots were fired?'

'If he was, then he must be a damned good shot,' she replied. 'The only blindfold other than mine that I saw was lying on the floor at his feet, next to the bed. But there was also a revolver lying on a side table within arm's reach of him, so *you* figure out what had just happened. Except, I suspect, you're just here to cover up for him.'

'In point of fact, your ladyship,' Percy replied solemnly, 'I can assure you that we're merely here to confirm what Scotland Yard was told by the local police.'

'Hmm,' was her doubtful response. 'Well, for my money that local inspector was too overawed by who he was dealing with. As soon as he learned that the only possible perpetrator of the deed was the heir to the throne, he was bowing and scraping. Since then, of course, that awful Albert has inherited his mother's crown, although she'll be turning in her grave to know that her son is such a dissolute, immoral wastrel!'

'Thank you most sincerely for your time, your ladyship,' Percy said courteously as he rose to his feet, and Jack followed suit, not sure whether or not protocol called for a bow. They left the drawing room swiftly and made their way down the hallway to the front door, where Jennings had the coach waiting.

'Home in time for what will hopefully prove to be a late supper,' Percy said with a smile. 'Well, what did you make of that, Jack?'

'She's a very handsome lady,' Jack replied.

'Yes, I could see that you were captivated,' Percy replied sardonically, 'but assuming that you were listening as well as watching, what vital facts emerged from what she told us?'

'That she didn't see who fired the shots, but assumed that it must have been the prince, because he was the only other person left alive in the room once she removed her blindfold.'

'Nothing else?'

'Such as?'

Percy sighed. 'For one thing, the fact that the valet who died was probably short enough to fit in that cabinet thing in the dressing room that I mentioned earlier, where he could have been kept for quite a while — even since the time when everyone else was having lunch outside, ahead of the hunt. And, of course, the sound of shotguns blasting in the trees a hundred yards or so away in the woods would have masked a mere revolver shot inside the house. So let's work on the theory that Wilson was killed at around lunchtime. That would account for the bloodstain on the linoleum in the dressing room, and the fact that he wasn't bleeding onto the bedchamber carpet. Men don't bleed after they've been dead for ten hours or so.'

'So who was responsible for all this?' Jack challenged him.

'Who was walking with a limp the following day, if you managed to absorb that while staring at the widow?' asked Percy.

'The prince's own valet, who'd got the day off, and had been in the hunting party,' Jack replied.

'And he could easily have sustained his injury by jumping down from the dressing room window,' Percy pointed out. 'Her ladyship saw the prince's valet for the last time that day shortly before the bunfight — what her ladyship referred to as "luncheon on the patio". But nobody would have noticed had he disappeared much earlier than that, since their eyes were glued to the doomed birds they were hunting.'

'But her ladyship *didn't* see him in the bedchamber when she removed her blindfold,' Jack objected, to a reproving tut from Percy.

'When she removed her blindfold and caught sight of her dead husband, she was, in her own words, "looking down a tunnel" — focused on the likelihood that she'd just become a widow. You could have produced a performing bear in there and she wouldn't have noticed.'

'So you believe that this missing royal valet may have been the culprit?'

'I'm not sure yet that Prince Albert *wasn't*,' Percy replied, 'but we need to keep our options open. At the very least there's another scenario opening up in my brain, for which I require corroboration from your good lady wife. And I'm hungry again.'

'Some things never change,' Jack muttered as he watched the cottages on the outskirts of Beaconsfield come into sight through the coach window.

CHAPTER SEVEN

Esther appeared at the front door as the coach came to a halt in front of it. She gestured for Jack and Percy to be as quiet as possible while they gave Jennings his instructions for the following morning, then ushered them inside.

'The children are all in their beds, and hopefully already asleep, although Annabelle may still be reading to Aunt Beattie,' Esther whispered. 'It's almost impossible to keep them apart, even when Annabelle should by rights be getting the same amount of sleep as Lily. I've had a late supper left for you in the oven, and hopefully the cottage pie won't have dried out too much.'

A short while later, the two men pushed their empty plates away and sat back contentedly on their dining room chairs.

'So what did you learn today?' Esther asked eagerly.

'Have you still got that crude diagram I drew the other day?' Percy asked.

Esther retrieved it from a drawer in the sitting room and returned to the dining room, laying it down on the table in front of Percy, along with several coloured pencils.

'We can now put names to the capital letters,' he told Esther. 'The one we called "A", as you already know, is Prince Albert. B is Lady Virginia Belvedere. We know from what she told us earlier today that she was blindfolded when she entered the bedchamber, led in there by C, who was her husband, Sir Rupert Belvedere. He ended up dead from a gunshot wound that can be proved to have come from the revolver on the side table by the bed, within Prince Albert's reach. We don't know yet whether or not he was blindfolded. The final person in that room, D, was a man called James Wilson, the valet employed by Sir Rupert. He was on loan to the prince because his normal valet, whose name we don't know yet, was given the day off in order to join the hunt. But keep him in mind.'

'Didn't you tell me last time that D also ended up dead?' Esther queried.

Percy nodded. 'Well remembered. The first and *only* theory from the local police was that he'd been shot at the same time as C, mainly because the witnesses all heard two shots and found two dead bodies. Also because the bullet found in his chest could be linked to the revolver on the bedside table. The revolver, you will recall, that had no finger impressions on it.'

'I think you told me all this already,' Esther replied. 'So what new facts have you unearthed?'

'We spoke to Lady Virginia at some length, and she confirmed that she wasn't wearing gloves when she went into the bedchamber. If she's telling the truth, then that appears to rule her out as the one who fired the fatal shots — or perhaps only *one* fatal shot, as I'll explain in a moment.'

'And did she tell you anything else of value?'

'Indeed she did,' Percy smiled. 'She claims that after she heard the second shot, she removed her blindfold, and was only able to focus on the sight of her dead husband lying on the floor. She said it was like looking down a tunnel. So she wasn't aware of anything else that might have been happening in the seconds immediately after the shootings — or perhaps only one shooting.'

'You've already hinted at that,' said Esther, slightly exasperated.

'We'll deal with it now,' said Percy. 'You will recall, from our previous conversation, that there was a dressing room-cum-lavatory leading off from the bedchamber, whose door was locked on the bedchamber side when the police tested it?'

'Yes, so what?'

'Well, it was one of those double-lock doors that you see in hotels that have adjoining rooms. There is a lock on *each* side, allowing the occupants of both rooms to either lock out the person in the adjoining room, or leave both doors unlocked to allow access between the two rooms. Well, we discovered that the door in question only appeared to be locked on the bedchamber side because the key had been left in it, and when one pushed the door, it wouldn't open.'

'So it was locked from the *other* side. What of it?' Esther replied with irritation.

Percy laughed. 'You concluded that without even seeing the door for yourself, whereas Jack had to have its significance demonstrated to him.'

'Get on with it,' Jack muttered, and Percy duly obliged.

'On the floor inside this dressing room we found what could well be a dried bloodstain. Since it seems the police never gained access to the room, they would not have seen this clear evidence that someone might have died in there. I therefore advance the theory that this was the case, and that since Sir Rupert was clearly still alive when he led his wife into the bedchamber, the person who died in that dressing room was the valet, Wilson.'

'Whose body was found in the bedchamber?' Esther queried. 'How does that fit whatever theory you're about to advance?'

'It's all to do with the *timing* of Wilson's death,' Percy explained. 'I haven't a clue why, but I believe that Wilson was shot earlier that day, and that his body was hidden in a long, low chest used for storing bed linen that was in the dressing room. Lady Virginia confirmed that Wilson was of below average height, *and*,' he added with a knowing smile, 'we learned from his lady friend — a parlourmaid employed in Bradenham House — that Wilson failed to keep an appointment with her on the afternoon of the day that his body ended up in the bedchamber. Conclusion? He was shot earlier and his body was concealed, then presented for public view at the same time that Sir Rupert was shot.'

'If you're correct, then the killer in both cases must be someone other than Prince Albert,' Esther concluded, and when Percy nodded his gleeful agreement, she added, 'This was what you were sent to conclude, wasn't it? Aren't you just pandering to your political masters?'

'I pander to *no-one*!' Percy insisted vehemently.

'Sorry,' said Esther in a small voice. 'So if we assume the presence of a third party, who is he, and why were there two shots heard in the bedchamber, if only one was required?'

'Reasoned like the professional you should have been,' Percy flattered her, 'so let's take those questions in reverse order. The need for a third shot was to convince the witnesses that both men had been shot at the same time. I believe that the culprit fired off a spare third shot into the ceiling, the floor, or wherever, and I'll need to have the room minutely inspected to confirm this at a later date.'

'But why was it necessary to shoot dead this valet earlier in the day?' Esther demanded.

'Again, I have no idea beyond the possibility that he caught the real culprit up to something in the dressing room.'

'And have you any idea who this mystery third person might be?'

'Jack can probably suggest a likely suspect,' Percy prompted, conscious that his nephew had not uttered a single word in relation to their joint operation — the one that Jack was officially leading.

Jack looked back at Percy in surprise, then collected himself. 'Ah, you mean the man with the limp. Lady Virginia told us that the prince's normal valet — the man whose name we don't even know yet — had the day off to attend the hunt that was the main purpose of the prince's visit to Bradenham House. He wasn't seen — by her, anyway — after the morning hunt, when everyone stopped for lunch on the terrace. But she saw him the following day, accompanying the prince as he climbed back into the carriage to return to London, and he was walking with a limp.'

'So?' Esther asked.

'What Uncle Percy failed to mention is that it's possible to escape from the dressing room adjoining the bedchamber by means of a window twelve feet from the ground. There's a drainpipe down one side, which may assist one's descent, but at a pinch one could jump the whole twelve feet and escape with only a twisted ankle.'

'So you're both concluding that this unnamed valet did the deed then escaped by way of this window?' Esther asked. 'Surely, if he'd been in the bedchamber to fire the fatal shot, or shots, he'd have been seen by either the prince or Lady Virginia, once they removed their blindfolds?'

'Remember what I said about Lady Virginia's immediate reaction to the sight of her husband lying dead on the carpet?' Percy interposed. 'She had eyes only for that. We haven't spoken to the prince yet, which is what I propose to remedy tomorrow, but suppose he reacted in the same way? The adjoining door to the dressing room was only two or three feet away from the bed, and was effectively *behind* him as he looked back into the room, so it might have been possible for this unnamed valet to slip the gun onto the side table, nip through the adjoining door, lock it on the dressing room side and descend to the ground through the window, spraining his ankle in the process.'

'It's all a bit — well, "conjectural", I suppose,' Esther reasoned, 'but it's a theory at least, and I appreciate you sharing all this with me. But what did you require my opinion on?'

'The intended victim,' Percy replied.

She frowned. 'Surely that was Sir Rupert?'

'One possibility, certainly,' Percy conceded, 'but we know of no obvious connection between the royal valet and Sir Rupert.'

'Perhaps he was paid to do it by Lady Virginia, to get rid of a husband much older than her, so she could inherit the estate?' Esther suggested.

Percy nodded. 'That's certainly more feasible than the suggestion that the intended victim was the valet Wilson, particularly since he was already dead by then, if my other theory's correct. But you're forgetting the obvious victim — the prince.'

'But he wasn't shot,' Esther objected.

'No, but he's been left to look like the culprit, hasn't he?'

'But is the prince — the king, as he is now — subject to the same laws as the rest of us?' Esther asked. 'Put another way, even if he's guilty, can he be prosecuted?'

'I can answer that,' Jack replied eagerly. 'There's something called "sovereign immunity" that prevents kings and queens from being prosecuted for a crime, which is no doubt why the local police didn't bother to follow up on what the bare facts suggested. But I'm not sure if it covers murder, or whether it gives immunity to mere princes, which is what our new king was at the time.'

'You're forgetting the German angle,' Percy reminded him. When Esther raised her eyebrows, he explained, 'When Melville first called us in, he mentioned the possibility that the finger was being pointed at Prince Albert by his nephew, Kaiser Wilhelm of Germany, with whom he doesn't enjoy the most loving of family relationships. Wilhelm's apparently suggesting that the prince shouldn't be allowed to inherit his mother's throne because he's a double murderer, although quite what Special Branch are expected to do to prevent that I've no idea. Our job is to find out what really happened, and perhaps absolve Albert.'

'And if you can't?' Esther challenged him.

Percy shrugged. 'The truth is what they'll get, whether they like it or not.'

'So let's go back to the problem of the three missing bullets from that revolver, whoever wielded it,' Esther suggested. 'As I understand your theory, the first shot was discharged in the dressing room earlier that day. Why did no-one hear it?'

'There was a group of idle layabouts firing shotguns at helpless grouse all morning, remember,' Percy replied. 'If you've ever been nearby when this outmoded and brutal pastime is taking place, then you'll know that the report from a revolver inside the house, while shotguns were being discharged nearby, would be as audible as a glass of water being emptied alongside a waterfall.'

'So the second and third shots occurred in the bedchamber,' Esther said, 'and only one of them was actually fatal — the one that killed Belvedere? Then the third one was shot off into the ceiling or somewhere, in order to make it look as if both deaths had occurred at the same time?'

'That's my theory,' Percy confirmed.

'And what does your theory have to say about how the body of the valet got from the linen chest in the back room into the bedchamber?'

'It doesn't have anything to say, at present,' Percy admitted with a furrowed brow, 'and I'm hoping that the prince can explain that.'

'You plan to question him?' Esther asked.

'Not without clearance from Melville, and of course the consent of His Majesty himself to speak with two grubby oiks from the Metropolitan Police.'

'How will you know if he's telling the truth?' Esther objected.

Percy smiled slowly. 'Years of experience, and an immunity from that feeling of inferiority that so many people experience when dealing with their so-called "social superiors". My entrenched socialist sympathies will, for once, stand me in great stead.'

'And we're going to speak with Melville tomorrow?' Jack asked.

'Indeed we are,' Percy confirmed, 'so I suggest that we get a good night's sleep. I've told Jennings to have the coach here by eight, so I hope that Polly's up to a full breakfast at seven.'

'So you can't yet exonerate His Majesty, is that what you're telling us?' Melville demanded as he sat alongside Assistant Commissioner Bruce behind the latter's desk in Scotland Yard shortly before eleven the following morning.

'That's not what I took our mission to be,' Percy replied. 'If you're asking whether or not we're any closer to learning the truth about what happened, then the answer is "yes", but there's one more witness we need to speak to. Following standard Procedures Manual strictures for once, we've left the putative suspect until last, when we have all the evidence available against which to assess his version of events.'

'Before we let you go blundering into an interview with our new king,' Melville growled, 'at least tell us what your findings are at this point.'

'Well,' Percy replied, 'it was certainly not a straightforward case of Prince Albert blasting off two fatal shots, one at his host for the weekend and the other at the valet on loan to him. There were *three* bullets missing from the revolver chamber, you may recall, and we believe that the first of those was discharged much earlier in the day, killing the valet hours before everyone seems to have assumed that he became the second victim of a murderous prince. We believe that this first body was hidden away until it was produced for inspection along with Sir Rupert's, and that the first shot that was heard by witnesses — the one that killed Sir Rupert — was in fact the second to come from that revolver. The third was fired harmlessly into the ceiling, or wherever, to make everyone believe that the two men were killed at the same time. We'll need a scientific team to visit the room in question in order to validate that theory, of course.'

'Before we do any of that,' Melville insisted, 'you can explain to me how the killer — assuming that it wasn't Prince Albert — managed to smuggle a body into the bedchamber without alerting the Prince's suspicions.'

'That's one of the reasons why we need to speak with the prince as the next stage in our investigations,' Percy replied.

Melville gave Bruce an anxious sideways look. 'Are you really prepared to take responsibility for these two blundering up to the palace to ask impertinent questions of our appointed monarch?'

'Our yet to be *anointed* monarch,' Percy corrected him, 'and one who may ascend to the throne with blood on his hands. And our questions will not be impertinent, merely relevant. Incidentally, do you happen to know if the prince is aware of the allegations being made against him by his far from beloved nephew?'

'See what I mean?' Melville demanded of Bruce. 'Enright Senior has all the tact of a charging bull, while the man officially in charge of this very delicate investigation is under your operational command. It will be on your head if we get a severe "please explain" from the Home Secretary.'

'This operation was dumped on us by you, with a request from the same Home Secretary that we pull the prince out of trouble,' Bruce replied crisply. 'If it goes wrong, I shall merely claim to have loaned you the manpower, with which you did what you chose to do. And it was you who requested the Enrights.'

'We're still here, by the way,' Percy reminded them both, 'and I can only advise you that unless we extract certain salient facts from the man who was there at the time, we'll get no further with providing you with a report, whether it's to your liking or not. I shall treat the king with all the respect to which he's entitled. My socialist principles do not in any way compromise my patriotism, or my desire to see this country well governed by a man who is at least popular with his subjects, if for all the wrong reasons.'

'Do we realistically have a choice?' Bruce asked.

Melville thought for a moment before shaking his head. 'No, damn it, we don't. But,' he added as he glared at Percy and Jack, 'there are many ways in which to interview witnesses — *witnesses*, mark you, not suspects — and I insist that you observe the niceties and palace protocols at all times. Show the man the reverence he's due as our monarch, and remember that he's not some old beggar you've just pulled off the street.'

'We shall be the soul of discretion,' Percy assured him.

Melville shook his head in a gesture of disbelief and asked if he might make use of the telephone on Bruce's desk.

After being connected to various individuals with increasingly pompous-sounding titles, to whom he spoke with appropriate degrees of sycophancy, he put down the phone and looked reluctantly at Percy.

'Three o'clock this afternoon. Best bib and tucker, and mind your manners. The palace will be expecting you.'

CHAPTER EIGHT

There was no disagreement regarding where Jack and Percy should spend at least part of their free time before taking their allocated coach to Buckingham Palace, and, seated at their preferred table in Tang Li's Chophouse on the Embankment an hour later, they both ordered the meat pie.

'Since we have a few moments to spare before our mouths become fully occupied, we should perhaps rehearse those questions that we'll be putting to the prince,' suggested Percy. 'You first.'

'We obviously need him to confirm whether or not he was blindfolded,' Jack began confidently, 'and if so, when precisely he took it off. Also whether he was wearing gloves, although someone in their bedchamber would have been unlikely to be doing so.'

'There's also the all-important question of what he saw when the blindfold, if it was on at all, came off,' Percy reminded him. 'Was he, like her ladyship, completely transfixed by the sight before him, to the exception of everything else? If so, would it have been possible for someone to place a recently discharged revolver onto the table slightly behind him, then make a hasty exit into the adjoining dressing room? Then there's the very interesting question of whether or not he'd had a valet in attendance immediately beforehand, and who it might have been. His own personal valet had the day off, remember, and the one who was supposed to have been replacing him ended up officially dead only minutes later. As I understand these matters, members of the royal family need constant assistance from manservants, so there was almost certainly one in attendance. If it was Wilson, what transpired between them? If it was his own personal valet, how did he explain his return to duty on a day off?'

'You're right,' Jack agreed. 'Those points never really occurred to me. I'm glad I have you to assist in my investigation.'

'So far you've been tagging along behind mine,' Percy replied wryly, 'but now let's eat.'

As three o'clock approached, Jennings drove the coach between the two members of the Household Cavalry who sat like statues on their mounts at the front entrance to Buckingham Palace, then brought it to a halt. A liveried footman stepped out of the shade to open the carriage door, and Jack and Percy stepped down from it, leaving Jennings to drive the coach into the stables yard as instructed. Another man in full livery stepped forward and enquired as to their business, and behind him stood a Guards officer with a ceremonial sword at his belt, just in case they didn't have any.

Jack showed the officer his police badge and said, 'His Majesty is expecting us, I believe.'

Without a word, the man turned and walked back into the cavernous front hall, which Jack took to be an indication that they should follow. Two staircases, three corridors and many hanging portraits later they came to a set of double doors guarded by more uniformed and heavily armed attendants, between whom stood a man in full naval uniform. He introduced himself as the duty royal equerry and asked to see proof of their identity. Jack produced his police badge again, and he and Percy were instructed to remain where they were while the equerry disappeared behind the double doors. A few moments later, he reappeared and gave them instructions.

'Bow when you enter the royal presence, do not take a seat unless and until invited, and keep it brief, since His Majesty has a busy schedule of audiences this afternoon.' He then tapped on the double doors, which were opened from the inside by what appeared to be another doorkeeper to the royal presence.

The doorkeeper led them through an outer chamber with portraits all over the walls, and filled with enough antique furnishings to equip several stately homes, until they reached another single door at the end. The man knocked three times on this door, then held it open for Jack and Percy to walk through as he announced, 'Gentlemen from Scotland Yard, Your Majesty.'

Jack led the way into the next room. There, seated on the most heavily padded armchair that Jack had ever seen, was the man he'd previously seen only in photographs. Prince Albert rose as Jack and Percy walked slowly towards him and bowed.

The photographs did not do justice to the man's height, nor did they adequately depict the almost aggressive paunch that protruded proudly from his waistcoat. He had a high forehead, a full black beard streaked with grey hair, and piercing hooded eyes that looked down at them inquisitively, like a hawk assessing its prey. Then he gave them a friendly nod as he acknowledged their bows and announced, "Protocol dictates that you cannot speak until I do, so consider that done, and tell me what you've learned about that dreadful business at Bradenham. You may both be seated for that purpose. Which of you is the senior officer?'

'That's me, Your Majesty,' Jack half croaked as nervous phlegm took command of his throat, which he cleared with a half cough. 'I am Chief Inspector Enright. The gentleman with me is Detective Sergeant Percival, and he's been the one collecting all the necessary information at the request of Superintendent Melville of Special Branch.'

'Who was no doubt given the job by the Home Secretary, who in turn received defamatory accounts of my alleged misbehaviour from the German Ambassador. He was no doubt encouraged by my despicable nephew. Have I assessed the situation correctly?'

'With remarkable acuity, if I may make so bold, Your Majesty,' Percy confirmed in a deferential tone that Jack found reassuring. 'We've been down to Bradenham House, and there conducted various enquiries, but there are certain facts only you can supply if we are to obtain a comprehensive understanding of what transpired that evening.'

'That's a somewhat excessive way of explaining that you've been told to clear my name, is it not?' the prince asked with a look of mild amusement.

Percy bowed his head slightly as he replied, 'With respect to both yourself and those who instruct me, Your Majesty, our mission was described as one to obtain the truth of what transpired. If it has the effect of clearing your name of any complicity in what occurred, then I for one shall be both proud of a job well done, and delighted that the royal reputation remains intact.'

The prince allowed himself a chuckle. 'My mother would have entertained no doubt of my guilt, of that I am sure. Since the tragic early death of my father, she regarded me as the Antichrist, and she was a most formidable lady. Did either of you meet her in your professional capacities?'

'I did,' Jack replied hesitantly. 'She gave me a medal.'

'Not for long service, to judge by your youthful appearance?'

'No, Your Majesty. It was for bravery, although I don't think I really deserved it.'

'The truly brave always think that,' the prince said with a smile, 'and I assume that your senior rank at such a young age is the reward for that bravery. But do you also possess the wisdom and modesty to allow a man older than you to conduct an investigation that's been nominally allocated to you?'

'Indeed I do,' Jack confirmed, 'and on this occasion, that man is Detective Sergeant Percival.'

'Very well,' the prince replied as he fixed his hooded gaze on Percy. 'What have you learned so far?'

'If I might begin by asking you to confirm the background circumstances as narrated to us by others?' Percy prompted. 'I believe that you were at Bradenham House at the invitation of Sir Rupert Belvedere, in order to take part in a weekend grouse shoot. After spending the Saturday engaged in that shoot, you were the guest of honour at a dinner. Have I got that much right?'

'Indeed you have,' the prince confirmed. 'So is there anything further you need to know up to that point?'

'Could you confirm that although you were accompanied by your personal valet, you in fact gave him the day off?'

'Also correct. Walter Ponsonby — the valet in question — is an excellent shot, having won prizes for his marksmanship during his days with the Coldstream Guards. All royal servants are former military officers, as you may know, and those closest to the family are drawn from the Guards regiments. Anyway, when we got there Ponsonby asked for leave to take part in the actual hunt, where, incidentally, he acquitted himself splendidly, potting a brace or two for himself. Then, as a reward for his loyal service, I gave him the rest of the weekend off as well, and the host very kindly lent me his own man, Wilson, to replace Ponsonby. Tragically, Wilson lost his life in the process.'

'But Ponsonby didn't quite escape that weekend unscathed, did he?' Percy asked. 'He ended up with a sprained ankle, according to a witness we spoke to.'

'Ah yes, well remembered,' said the prince. 'Apparently he went for a walk in the grouse coppice after dark, while we were all having dinner, and he tripped on an exposed tree root. That was his explanation, anyway, for why he was limping when he showed up the following morning, but I wouldn't be surprised to learn that he'd been amorously engaged with one of the serving girls, with which the Bradenham estate seemed to be well endowed.'

'Presumably Ponsonby had to return to duty the following morning because Wilson — the Belvedere valet — had been shot during the incident the night before?' Percy asked.

The prince's face clouded. 'Actually, he'd been obliged to do that *before* Wilson was killed, which was why I was so surprised to see Wilson lying there when I took off my blindfold.'

'When was that?' Jack asked.

The prince shot him an irritated look. 'When I heard the gunshots, obviously.' He turned back to Percy and asked, 'Where were we?'

Jack opted for silence for the remainder of their audience.

'You mentioned that Ponsonby was on duty *before* Wilson lost his life,' Percy prompted.

'Yes, that was it. Earlier that evening, when I withdrew to my room in order to dress for dinner, I was surprised to find Ponsonby in attendance. He explained that Wilson was indisposed, but that since I'd been generous enough to allow him to take part in the hunt he was more than happy to resume duties. He was still there when I returned to the room to engage in a silly wager that we'd agreed on downstairs when we'd all had far too much to drink.'

'I don't require the precise terms of that wager,' Percy told him tactfully.

The prince chuckled. 'Perhaps as well, but it *did* require me to be blindfolded, and when I went back up to my room in order to divest myself of my somewhat cumbersome evening jacket and cravat, Ponsonby was there, and he was the one who tied my blindfold.'

'He just happened to have one available?' Percy queried cynically.

The prince shook his head. 'Obviously not. We made use of a napkin that had been laid out on the side table, no doubt by a chambermaid when preparing the room ahead of my visit.'

'Regarding that side table,' Percy began, since the opportunity had presented itself, 'I was told that it had been moved from one side of the bed to the other.'

'Correct,' the prince confirmed. 'I'm accustomed to having it on the right-hand side as you look at the bed. I was quite happy to leave it on the left, but when I got up there for the blindfolding, I noticed that Ponsonby had taken it upon himself to move it, in accordance with my preferred practice. Typical Ponsonby — such an eye for detail.'

'Since we're on the subject of the blindfold,' Percy continued, 'did you have it on when the shots were fired?'

'Yes, of course.'

'And how long had it been in place *before* you heard the shots?'

'Difficult to tell,' the prince replied. 'You know how it is — when one sense is taken from you, the others become more acute. I could no longer see, so my hearing was enhanced, and of course I was awaiting the arrival of what was supposed to be the first of several ladies for me to identify. In fact, I thought I heard one of them arriving — a sort of shuffling noise that I took to be the sound of the door from the hallway opening. Then it went quiet again, and just when I was about to call out to Ponsonby to enquire whether or not the game had been abandoned, I heard the hallway door opening, and the swish of a lady's gown. That must have been Lady Virginia, of course, because then I heard two loud shots, one immediately after the other, and I pulled off my blindfold. I could clearly see Belvedere's valet lying on the carpet, and then when Lady Virginia screamed I looked across at her, and became aware that Rupert Belvedere had also been shot. I asked what had just happened, but she went all hysterical, and then other people rushed into the room and it became quite chaotic. I was conscious that I was only half dressed, and made hurried efforts to put my evening jacket back on.'

'Assisted by Ponsonby?' Percy suggested.

The prince shook his head. 'No idea where he got to, but then the Belvedere steward came in and announced that he was calling the police. He stayed with me until they arrived, and I told them what I could. They hung around for the next few hours until I complained that I was weary, and they left in order that I might finally get to bed.'

'Might I ask if you were wearing gloves?' Percy asked.

'I had been earlier, but the nature of the wager I'd agreed to meant that I had to have my hands unencumbered, so I took my gloves off and handed them to Ponsonby to put in my travelling valise. You're seeking to clarify why my finger impressions weren't on that revolver, aren't you? The police officer who was in charge seemed to set great store by that, and I heard him say to another officer that even if my finger impressions were there, it wouldn't signify much, since it was my revolver anyway. Except it wasn't.'

Jack's jaw dropped, and Percy's eyes narrowed as he sought clarification.

'How do you know it wasn't yours?' he asked.

The prince's face took on a slightly exasperated expression as he replied, 'Why would I bring my revolver on a weekend shoot? We had shotguns, certainly, and I brought my two best Purdeys with me, but no revolver. And in any case, mine has a six-shot capacity — a more recent model Webley — whereas I'm told that the weapon used had capacity for five shots.'

'Did you tell the officer in charge of the initial investigation that it wasn't your weapon?'

'He didn't ask, and it never occurred to me that I might be suspected of having fired it. I *am* a suspect, aren't I?'

'Not according to the local police, whose enquiries we've been asked to follow up,' Percy assured him, 'particularly since your finger impressions were not found on the weapon.'

'Then whose were?'

'Nobody's, so far as I'm aware,' Percy told him. 'If I might also enquire about the dressing room and bathroom that adjoined the bedchamber — did you have occasion to make use of either of them that evening?'

'Only the dressing room, prior to going down to dinner,' the prince replied. 'When I came back up in order to take part in the wager, I handed my outer jacket and cravat to Ponsonby with instructions to put them in my travelling bag, which was in the room with us. As for the bathroom, there was a chamber pot provided for my convenience under the bed, and I employed it before finally settling down for the night, not that I got much sleep. The following morning, it was Ponsonby who woke me up with a pot of tea, and arranged for a rather sad-looking parlourmaid to bring me some toast and eggs.'

'The girl in question was in a romantic relationship with the dead valet, Wilson,' Percy told him.

The prince nodded. 'Poor girl, but I left her a generous gratuity for her excellent service. A pretty thing she was, from memory.'

'Do you recall what happened to the blindfold you'd been wearing?'

'Ponsonby found it lying at the side of the bed the next morning. I must have dropped it when I became aware of the shootings.'

'Finally,' said Percy, 'can you think of anyone who might have wanted Sir Rupert Belvedere dead?'

'Not really,' said the prince. 'He was a frightful bore, of course, always droning on about his steelworks up north, but my mother always encouraged me to ingratiate myself with those who are the source of the nation's wealth. Then there was that awful German idiot he'd invited along — some sort of industrial chemist who was going to revolutionise British steelmaking, according to him. He also had that insufferable manner about him that so many of his race seem to be afflicted with — so smug and confident, always quick to go one better than everyone else. He was the one who took what had until then been idle chatter about my alleged bedroom conquests and converted it into a stupid wager that I doubted my capacity to win. But by then he'd irritated me to the point at which I was determined to prove him to be a pretentious windbag.'

Percy was about to rise and bow his way out with suitable thanks, when the prince raised a hand to detain him.

'Let me ask *you* something, Sergeant. Do you have any evidence that might identify someone who's determined to smear my name in order to prevent my coronation?'

'No, Your Majesty,' Percy replied. 'One name *has* been suggested, but I have no evidence that would give it any credence at this stage.'

'Then *find* some!' the prince urged him. 'I want the Kaiser's name dragged through the same mud that he's obviously trying to bury me in. And now this audience is at an end.'

A short while later, Jack and Percy were back in the coach that Jennings had been instructed to bring to the front door. 'Not quite the refined gentleman of royal blood that the authorities would have us believe,' Percy chuckled.

'But is he lying?' Jack asked.

Percy thought for a moment, then replied, 'My instincts say not, but that's a long way from proving his innocence. So where would you suggest we go next with our enquiries?'

'The missing Ponsonby has no doubt got certain information we'd find of value,' Jack replied.

'And, I suspect, a very good reason for not supplying it, if he were forced to tell the truth,' added Percy. 'I'll need to get Melville to dig into his background, clearly. And while he's at it, he can get me some inside information on that German industrial type who seems to have engineered the prince into a compromising situation — whether to have Belvedere murdered, or simply to drop Prince Albert in it remains to be seen. But this is by no means over.'

'Have we finished for the day?' Jack asked hopefully.

'We have,' Percy confirmed. 'I've instructed Jennings to drive us home — by which I mean Watford, for another of Polly's delightful dinners.'

CHAPTER NINE

On the following morning, Wednesday, Jack and Percy allowed themselves a leisurely breakfast before climbing into the coach driven by a smiling Jennings, who'd also enjoyed the late start. It was approaching the lunch hour, which promised another leisurely walk down the Embankment to Tang Li's, when the two men reported back to Melville and Bruce on the outcome of their audience with Prince Albert.

'Well, at least so far, we haven't received any complaint from the Home Secretary regarding the manner in which you interviewed the prince,' Melville told them sourly, 'so we can only assume that Percy was on his best behaviour. So how went things, and what did you learn?'

'Several things of considerable value in the overall investigation,' Percy announced. 'In particular, we can confirm that the prince was not wearing gloves at the time of the shooting, and that the revolver found on the side table was not his.'

There was a silence before Melville turned to Bruce and asked, 'Who alleged that it was?'

'No-one, actually,' Percy replied before Bruce could fumble a response. 'It was assumed by the local police that it belonged to the prince, and they never thought fit to ask him to confirm that fact. In fact, as he rightly pointed out, why would he have brought it with him on a hunting weekend when he was already equipped with shotguns? Anyway, he claims his revolver is one of the more recent six-chamber ones, whereas the one on the side table was a five-chamber one.'

'Then whose was it?' Melville demanded grumpily.

'I was rather hoping that you could discover that for us,' Percy said. 'Don't they have serial numbers?'

'I believe so,' Melville confirmed, 'but where is the weapon now?'

'Presumably the Buckinghamshire Police still have it,' Jack suggested. 'We were never shown it when we visited the station at High Wycombe, but it would be held as part of the evidence in the case, would it not?'

'I'll have someone enquire,' Bruce volunteered as he made a quick note on the pad in front of him.

'What else did you learn?' Melville asked.

'Interestingly, although Prince Albert had given his man — Walter Ponsonby — the rest of that weekend off, Ponsonby had put himself back on duty by the time the prince was ready to dress for dinner,' Percy replied. 'He claimed that the Belvedere valet, Wilson, was indisposed. However, I believe Wilson was almost certainly dead at that time. Anyway, it was Ponsonby who tied a blindfold around the prince's head in furtherance of the grubby wager that had been agreed. Incidentally, it would also seem to have been Ponsonby who had earlier moved the side table, on which the revolver was later discovered, to the side of the bed closest to the communicating door to the dressing room.'

'This is presumably significant?' Melville prompted.

'It is indeed. I shall reveal why in a moment,' Percy replied with the air of a conjurer. 'If I might continue?'

'Yes, yes, get on with it,' Melville urged, and Percy obliged.

'Another *very* significant fact revealed by the prince was that while he was sitting, blindfolded, awaiting the arrival of the first lady for him to identify, he heard what he described as "a sort of shuffling noise" that he initially took to be the entrance of that first lady. However, the much clearer sound of Lady

Virginia's entrance, consisting of the swishing of her skirts, was heard seconds later, just before the two shots rang out. My developing theory is that what the prince heard was the body of Wilson being dragged from the dressing room into the bedchamber, ready to be on display as the second victim.'

Melville's eyes widened. 'Anything else?'

'Perhaps the most significant fact of all is regarding how Ponsonby got away with it. Immediately following the two gunshots, when the prince removed his blindfold, he first became aware of Wilson's body lying on the floor, and was then distracted by Lady Virginia's hysteria, and the realisation that Belvedere had also been shot. In relation to both matters, his attention would clearly have been focused on the area of the room immediately in front of him. The bedside table, and the door to the adjoining dressing room, were both effectively behind him, and it's just feasible that Ponsonby had time to slip the revolver onto the side table, then escape through the adjoining door and lock it behind him. The prince had no recollection of where Ponsonby got to after the shootings, and so far as we're aware the police had no idea he had even been present, and therefore didn't interview him. My theory is that he made his exit by way of the drainpipe running down the outside wall through the bathroom window, spraining his ankle in the process. His excuse for that the following morning was that he'd been for a late-night stroll in the woods. After his master had somehow been involved in a double murder, mark you!'

'You clearly suspect this Ponsonby chappie,' Melville observed.

'Wouldn't you, based on the facts I've just outlined?' Percy replied. 'What do we know about him?'

'Bugger all, at this stage,' Melville replied, 'except that he must be ex-military, as virtually all royal servants are. In fact, those closest to the monarch himself are usually former Guardsmen.'

'A Coldstream Guard, in Ponsonby's case,' Jack volunteered. 'I remember the prince mentioning that, and my son has a whole army of tin ones, so the name was familiar to me.'

'And the prince mentioned what a good shot Ponsonby was,' Percy added. 'He seems to have been one of the more successful of those slaughtering helpless grouse that morning, before disappearing at around lunchtime.'

'Perhaps you should investigate this Ponsonby cove,' Bruce suggested.

'You most *definitely* should,' Percy put in, 'but not just him.'

'Who else?' Melville demanded. 'Surely you've pointed the finger at the likely candidate for the one who fired the revolver?'

'Yes, but why?' Percy challenged him. 'And for that matter, who made it possible?' Both Melville and Bruce stared back at him blankly, so he went on, 'Both Lady Virginia and the prince were understandably reticent about the grubby details of the wager that made it possible for the deed to be carried out. But ask yourself how it was possible for such a complex and tightly timed incident to be meticulously planned in advance. If someone hadn't manoeuvred Sir Rupert and Lady Belvedere into such a contrived situation, knowing that Ponsonby was already waiting, ready to take full advantage of two blindfolded dupes being in position, it could never have been pulled off.'

Melville finally lost patience. 'For God's sake, Enright, take that smug look off your face and just tell us!'

'How did the German ambassador know that the purpose of the wager that had been agreed was to see if the prince could recognise a woman he'd once bedded while both he and that woman were blindfolded?'

'We believe he was told by the Kaiser,' Bruce reminded him.

'And who told the Kaiser?' Percy prompted. 'Someone who spoke German, perhaps?'

After another brief silence, Bruce tentatively suggested, 'Von Huber?'

'Yes, von Huber,' Percy confirmed. 'From what Superintendent Bruce first told us — which has been confirmed by the prince — it was von Huber who goaded Prince Albert to the point where he agreed to the whole business, even down to being blindfolded. What I *don't* know at this stage was whether his agenda was the death of Sir Rupert, or the compromising of Prince Albert. But if it wasn't the latter, why did he bother advising the Kaiser? And did the Kaiser himself order the entire business?'

'We certainly know that he saw the opportunity to benefit from it,' Melville said with a nod, 'but are you saying that it's still possible for the real target to have been Belvedere? If so, why not simply arrange for him to be assassinated in a less complicated way? A sniper hidden in his woods, or poison in his wine or something?'

'Precisely,' Percy agreed. 'My money's still on the prince being the target, but we need to explore the links between the Kaiser, von Huber and Belvedere. We know that von Huber had wormed his way into Belvedere's company by way of some promise to assist in his steel business, but was he sent to do that by one of Britain's biggest rivals in the steel industry worldwide?'

'My God,' Melville muttered, 'this business has suddenly opened into a whole maze of possibilities, some of which have grave implications for our economy as well as the smooth succession of our new monarch.'

'And while I'm often accused of reading only the racing page,' Percy replied, 'I read enough of the rest of our newspapers to know that our current relationship with Germany is, shall we say, somewhat strained in *both* departments.'

It fell silent again, until Melville announced, 'I clearly need to instigate further enquiries by my own people in order to get you the answers you need, Percy. But even at this stage it looks as if you've revealed a far more serious and deep-rooted problem than the mere murder of a steelworks owner and his valet. Can you hold yourself ready to move in other directions once I get the information you require?'

'Of course,' Percy confirmed. 'I'd welcome the opportunity to return to my normal professional activities, and I have no doubt that Jack needs to catch up with what's been happening in his little corner of the Met, so we'll await further instructions from you. And now, in the hope that there's still meat pie on the menu at our favourite lunch establishment, we'll take our leave.'

Over what was almost a celebratory lunch at Tang Li's, it was agreed that Jennings would take Percy back to his office in Hackney for the afternoon. He would then collect Jack from the Met headquarters, together with Percy, at five o'clock and drive both men back to Watford, before returning home himself until the two men had further need of his services.

Shortly after six-thirty that evening, when Jack and Percy alighted from the coach at the front door of The Lodge, they were made aware of another matter that seemed to require investigation.

'Go and listen to what Aunt Beattie has to tell you about what happened to her today,' Esther told them. 'I've heard it three times already. Hopefully she'll shut up about it once she's unburdened herself to you two, although quite what she thinks you can do about it, I've no idea.'

They found Beattie seated on the settee in front of the fire, with one arm protectively around Annabelle's shoulder. 'It was quite outrageous!' Beattie exclaimed. 'A man and woman knocked on the front door at about eleven this morning, asking to speak with the householder. Alice let them in, not realising who they were or what they wanted, and I explained that both Esther and yourself were at work. Then they asked about Annabelle, and I told them that she was at school. I could hardly believe my ears when I heard what came next.'

Neither Jack nor Percy needed to prompt her, since the pause was of the dramatic variety, so they waited politely for the storm that seemed imminent.

'They claimed to be from some organisation calling itself the "Church of England Moral Welfare Association", which of course got my back up immediately. No single church can claim the monopoly on moral welfare, and certainly not *that* bunch of secret papists!'

Beattie had been brought up in the Methodist tradition, her father having been a lay preacher on the North London circuit. As she'd progressed through her mature years, she'd become more doggedly opposed to the more formal Church of England establishment, which often seemed to celebrate the glory of God with a pomp and ritual that smacked of the old ways before the Reformation. Percy recognised the warning signs of a full sermon about to be inflicted upon them, and sought to keep things moving by enquiring, 'What did they want?'

'They were asking about Annabelle, the impudent wretches!' Beattie replied, clearly outraged. 'They said that they'd heard she was an orphan who'd been kidnapped from a circus, and was living as a serving girl to a large family. I soon put them right on both matters and showed them the door, with a few sharp words about how belonging to the Church of England placed *them* in more moral danger than Annabelle was exposed to in this house!'

'I can imagine,' Percy chuckled, 'but how did they know about the circus?'

'I have no idea, obviously,' Beattie insisted, 'but I made it abundantly clear that it had been her stepfather who'd arranged for her to be kidnapped and enticed into performing there, and that you and Jack had been the ones who'd rescued her. As for her being a servant girl, I showed them all the books that she's read since being here, and assured them that her future spiritual welfare was assured, but not in *their* ungodly shrine to Popery!'

Jack was thinking deeply as he asked, 'Did they give you any idea of where they'd got the information about the circus?'

'No,' Beattie replied, 'and I never asked. I was too busy giving them a piece of my mind, let me tell you!'

Jack thought back to when he had first met Annabelle. Two years previously, there had been an attempt to ruin the private school that Lily and Annabelle attended, of which Esther was the deputy headmistress. A series of acts of vandalism, accompanied by rumours that the school was haunted by a vengeful spirit seeking to abduct a child, had culminated in Annabelle being enticed away from the school and invited to join a troupe of dancers in a travelling circus. The person behind the abduction had been her own stepfather, who'd had no time for her, and whom she'd detested. He in turn had been acting on behalf of a man from the unfortunate past of the school's headmistress and proprietor, Esther's employer Emily Allsop. The man had been obsessed with taking revenge against her.

Jack and Percy had joined forces to rescue Annabelle from what could have been an uncertain future, but in the aftermath of the uncovering of the plot, Annabelle's stepfather had murdered her mother, leaving her an orphan when he was duly hanged. Since her only friend in the world had been their daughter Lily, Jack and Esther had provided Annabelle with a new home in which she had blossomed and regained her confidence.

Annabelle and Beattie now enjoyed an 'aunt and niece' relationship, which Beattie was hoping might become more like a 'grandmother and granddaughter' bond. Little wonder that she was now bristling at the suggestion that Annabelle was in some sort of moral danger.

'Whoever told those interfering busybodies about the circus not only knew that Annabelle had needed rescuing from there, but also chose to twist the facts,' Percy observed. 'Let's hope that it's not another vendetta against the school.'

Their gloomy thoughts were interrupted by Esther rushing into the sitting room, pale-faced and breathless.

'It's Bertie!' she gasped. 'He was brought home in a coach from his exercises in that Boy's Battalion group, and he's injured his leg!'

Jack and Percy followed her back out into the front hall, where a green-faced Bertie was leaning on a gold-topped walking cane, being fussed around by Alice, and insisting that he didn't need to go to his bed.

'What happened?' Jack demanded.

Bertie looked shamefaced as he explained, 'I was scaling the Heights of Abraham on a rope when I lost my grip and fell. I landed a bit funny, and now my ankle hurts. But the Major gave me this cane and sent me home in his coach. He said I'll be back to normal in a few days.'

'What on earth are the Heights of Abraham?' Jack demanded.

'It's what I pretended I was climbing,' said Bertie, 'like the cliffs that were captured by the British led by General Wolfe against the French in Quebec. Except it was actually the barn wall at the side of the Major's house in the park.'

'You mean to tell us that the Major — by whom I think you mean the Earl of Essex — encouraged a nine-year-old boy to attempt to climb a wall on a rope?' Jack asked in disbelief.

Bertie nodded. 'It was the exercise he set us today. He told us all about the Heights of Abraham, and said that it was something we needed to learn if we're going to be proper soldiers.'

'That's it!' Jack shouted. 'I *knew* it was mistake to allow you to join that club that the earl established! He's just trying to get recruits for a regiment that can throw away their lives in the futile service of king and country. You're not going back there ever again, understand?'

'He's clearly not going *anywhere* for a day or two,' Esther pointed out. 'Not even to school, I imagine. Can you walk at all, Bertie?'

'I can if I lean on this cane that the Major loaned me,' Bertie replied, 'but it's very sore.'

'Very well,' Esther replied. 'Your father will help you into the kitchen, and I'll get Polly to cook you your favourite sausages for supper. Then it's off to bed with you, and we'll decide what's to happen tomorrow when we see what a night's rest can achieve. Jack, help him into the kitchen, would you?'

'He's still not going back to that recruitment camp,' Jack muttered as he lifted Bertie clean off his feet and carried him through to the kitchen, followed by a still fussing Alice and a very concerned Esther.

CHAPTER TEN

The remainder of the week passed without any further contact from either Bruce or Melville, so Jack and Percy slipped back into their normal activities, which seemed unexciting compared with the Belvedere matter. For Jack it was the long-delayed opportunity to conduct two recruitment interviews that had been left to him. Both involved unusual applicants — two young men who seemed unlikely recruits for uniformed beat duty on the crime-infested streets of the capital.

The first was the son of a Church of England minister from Bow, who had grown up bemused and saddened by the crime and poverty in the surrounding streets. He had been 'called', as his father put it, to play his part in making the streets safer for his honest, decent, but struggling neighbours to live their lives without fear. The second was the younger son of a wealthy farmer from Surrey, who wanted more excitement out of life than attending stock sales, meeting with estate managers and hosting local livestock shows.

They were both starkly middle-class and unlikely additions to the rugged band of those who patrolled London's streets, mixing with criminals, prostitutes and purveyors of illegal substances. But it was the accepted view within the higher echelons of the Met that well educated, articulate and highly motivated recruits from such privileged backgrounds would in due course rise up through the ranks and enhance the quality of senior management, while in the meantime raising the public image of those attired in blue serge constables' uniforms. Since Jack had himself joined the Met as something of an oddity — the grammar school-educated son of a wealthy insurance broker from Essex, and the nephew of established Met detective Percy Enright, himself the son of a middle-class doctor — he had been regarded as the best man possible to recruit others like him. This was why he had been taken out of the operational side of Scotland Yard in order to occupy the specially created role of Chief Inspector, Recruitment and Manpower.

For Percy, the temporary reprieve from the investigation was an opportunity to catch up with several commissions that had landed on his desk in his absence from his Hackney office. But none presented him with any great challenge, and in one sense it was a shame to take the money. He was able to cut significant corners while fulfilling a commission from the suspicious wife of a milk roundsman in outlying Wood Green, who believed that her husband was having an affair with one of his customers. Percy followed the man one day, posing as a 'knocker-upper' — a well-established occupation for elderly men or married women, who were employed by clients to knock on their bedroom windows to wake them when it was time to rise for work. This enabled Percy to wander, seemingly in a pre-determined pattern, but in fact following the milk roundsman until he saw him spend thirty minutes in a particular house in a side street.

Percy then positioned himself outside this same house for two more days, posing this time as a blind beggar, to satisfy himself that this was indeed the lady with whom the milkman divided his affections. Then he switched to a third assumed identity, this time as an official employed on the 1901 Census, collecting data on the occupancy of each house on the thirty-first of March. By late on Friday afternoon, he was able to complete a report to his client containing the name of the lady, the fact that she was a widow in her late forties, her address, and the two occasions on which it had taken her husband over thirty minutes to deliver a pint of milk.

The second commission, and one that gave Percy greater personal satisfaction, involved advising the owner of a large and busy public house in Finsbury Park that his senior barmaid was indeed stealing from him. Not by taking from the box behind the main bar that was used to collect all the takings, which would have been too obvious, but by failing to put the money in there in the first place. By sitting at the bar with a drink, Percy was able to watch carefully as the lady in question, with whose description he'd been provided, slipped handfuls of coins into her copious apron at busy times when the other servers behind the bar were engaged with customers. Percy calculated that the amount he saw the lady steal in one evening alone more than justified his fee.

But when the weekend came around, both Jack and Percy admitted to being bored, and were more than ready to be launched back into their enquiries into the Belvedere Scandal, as Melville insisted on calling it.

Saturday was wet and miserable as spring announced its early arrival, and everyone was confined indoors, but the sun reappeared in time for breakfast on Sunday morning. Bertie was finally given an outlet for his restless disposition and allowed into the open space behind The Lodge.

His sprained ankle had proved susceptible to the pressure bandages that Esther had applied, and although he still needed to take care while descending the stairs from his bedroom, he could walk freely along flat surfaces, provided that he made use of the cane that had been loaned to him by the earl. Jack had a walking stick of his own, retained from the days when he'd been recovering from a broken leg acquired in the course of duty in the East End, and he gave that to Bertie instead.

After demonstrating that it was every bit as good as the gold-topped cane, Bertie was allowed outdoors for long enough to return the cane to the earl with grateful thanks, and with Jack's stern instruction that he would not be taking part in the activities of the Boys' Battalion for the foreseeable future. In order to ensure that Bertie delivered this message, and to keep him company during the several hundred yards in each direction that he would be required to limp with the aid of Jack's cane, Annabelle was assigned duties as his companion. Lily declined the opportunity because she was too busy making herself a new smock for school wear, and the remaining Enright children were too young. In addition, there was a growing 'brother and sister' bond between Bertie and Annabelle that could on this occasion be employed to good effect.

Monday morning saw Jack and Percy go their separate ways, but not for long. At around ten o'clock that morning Jack was told that Melville wished to see them both in Bruce's office at two o'clock that afternoon, and he made use of the fact that Percy had recently had a telephone installed in his business office. After a hearty lunch at Tang Li's they reported for duty in Bruce's office, to find Melville already there, and wearing a smug smile that he might have borrowed from Percy.

'My enquiries have yielded several leads,' he announced, 'so be prepared to make good use of them. First of all, the weapon that was used to kill both Belvedere and his valet.'

'Stolen?' Percy asked.

Melville shrugged. 'Missing, anyway — from the armoury inside the Tower of London several years ago.'

'It's taken them *this* long to discover that it's missing?' Percy asked sharply.

'They knew it was missing, obviously, but were unable to locate it by the time they discovered that fact. It was seemingly issued as part of a handful given to a gun club operating within the Tower. All above board, and run by the Constable of the Tower in order to improve the arms capability of those Guards regiments that take it in turn to actually guarantee the security of the Tower while those Beefeater chaps swan around looking important.'

'Was one of those regiments by any chance the Coldstream Guards?' Jack asked eagerly.

Melville smiled. 'Well guessed, Jack, but it's even more suspicious than that.' Since neither Jack nor Percy invited him to continue, he asked, 'Why haven't you asked me more about that gun club?'

'Because if it's important, you'll no doubt tell us anyway, and we didn't want to spoil your fun,' Percy growled.

Melville shot him a look that could kill before continuing, 'The Constable of the Tower, both at the time when the gun went missing, and now, is Sir Frederick Stephenson, Colonel in Chief of the Coldstreams. Can either of you see where this is going?'

'You don't suspect *him* of stealing revolvers from the Tower Armoury, surely?' Jack piped up before he had time to prevent himself looking foolish.

Melville shook his head. 'Of course not, but of particular interest is the fact that he left the running of the gun club to his adjutant, who until some eighteen months ago was — guess who?'

'Ponsonby,' Percy replied in a bored tone. 'It only makes sense that this was where you were heading with your irritating guessing game. So you believe that Ponsonby stole the revolvers — is that your conclusion? If so, why wasn't he

117

drummed out of the regiment and gaoled for the rest of his natural life?'

'It's not so simple,' Melville explained. 'The loss of the weapons didn't become obvious until long after Ponsonby had left the service of the constable for entirely different, but interesting, reasons. Then they only realised that four revolvers were missing when they did a random stock-take. It seems that record-keeping inside the armoury had become a little slack, and it's since been improved, but during the relevant period it was possible for the weapons to have been signed back in using a forged signature. "Signature" is in fact a polite way of describing what was little better than a scrawl. But since the books seemed straight, it wasn't until a random counting of stock took place that the absence of the weapons was revealed. The upshot of that is that we don't know precisely when the weapons were stolen, only that they're missing. More importantly, we can't sheet home the theft to Ponsonby — all we know for certain is that on the day when he was in attendance on the prince, the weapon used to kill Belvedere and Wilson was one of those stolen from the Tower.'

In the silence that followed, Percy remembered something. 'You hinted that the circumstances in which Ponsonby ceased being the bag carrier for the Constable of the Tower were of interest. Care to expand?'

'I was going to anyway,' Melville replied testily. 'It seems that the gun club wasn't the only little gathering that Ponsonby organised during his time as the constable's adjutant. He was also the convenor of a covert gambling operation that caused considerable unrest and enmity between the men. Seemingly Ponsonby is an inveterate gambler, and a former member of a gentleman's club across St James's Park from the Wellington

Barracks in which the Coldstream Guards have their regimental headquarters. More of that in a moment.'

'Is that how he came to leave the Tower?' Jack asked.

Melville nodded. 'Indeed it was. Colonel Stephenson was getting more and more concerned about the unsettling effect of Ponsonby's gaming club on the men stationed at the Tower. When the prince's former valet retired, thereby creating a vacancy, he encouraged Ponsonby to apply for it, hinting that if he didn't he'd be transferred back to general Guard duties anyway because the adjutant's role needed to be rotated.'

'So Ponsonby became Prince Albert's valet,' Percy concluded. 'But why is Ponsonby a "former" member of this gentlemen's club — or can I guess? Gambling debts?'

'That's for you to find out, Percy,' Melville replied coldly. 'I can't be expected to do everything, and I've given you both plenty to go on. The club in question is "Montague's", and it's located in St James's Street. Over to you.'

'What about that German man?' Jack asked. 'Von something or other?'

'Von Huber,' Melville supplied. 'He's an interesting case, but I'm not sure we can link him with Ponsonby at this stage. Belvedere certainly, but we already knew that. What I *can* tell you is that von Huber is listed as a trade ambassador of the German Government, and is therefore covered by diplomatic immunity. Tread carefully there — preferably don't tread at all. He's an industrial chemist by trade, and his association with Belvedere was an innocent one, if you count industrial espionage as innocent. But I'm sure you don't want a lecture on the current state of the British steel industry.'

'I always find your lectures so informative,' Percy replied drily. 'Before we erase von Huber from the blackboard, please elaborate on the nature of his "industrial espionage". Or is it beyond your technical remit?'

'If you insist,' Melville sighed, 'but don't then complain that you're bored. You presumably already know, from your dedication to newspaper pages containing more than the racing results, that Britain and Germany are competing against each other to achieve dominance in the production of warships. Well, that requires steel, and modern industrial chemists are falling over each other to improve production methods. The current standard production technique is what's known as the "Bessemer" system, and it's ideal for the production of ship's plating, which is obviously of considerable assistance in our race to outgun Germany's navy. But there is said to be a refinement of the system originating in Germany, known, if my memory serves me correctly, as the "Siemens-Martin" process, which allows for more steel and less scrap, and is therefore both more productive and more economical. It seems that Belvedere had invited von Huber to be his guest in the hope of acquiring an introduction to this system, and that von Huber had played along in order to learn how much Belvedere had learned, and — it may be surmised — to put him on the wrong track towards employing it. Why else would von Huber have been given diplomatic cover by his embassy, and seemingly afforded such high status by his own government? Our conclusion is that the Kaiser had sent him here in order to prejudice any development in British steel-making.'

'When you first briefed us,' Percy reminded him, 'you intimated that Belvedere's business interests were waning. Now you seem to be telling us that his steelworks are of some importance to Britain's economic rivalry with Germany. Which is it?'

'It's true that Belvedere Metals are currently in something of a decline,' Melville confirmed, 'which is precisely why Belvedere was looking for some way of gaining an advantage over his industry rivals, and why Germany was motivated to prevent him acquiring this new smelting system.'

'So is it still possible that Belvedere was the real target?' Jack ventured.

For once Melville looked uncomfortable. 'We cannot be certain,' he admitted, 'but clearly, once the deed had been done in the presence of the prince, and duly reported back to the Kaiser, the possibility of a double advantage presented itself.'

'And have you uncovered any possible links between von Huber and Ponsonby?' Percy asked. 'Or was *that* serendipitous as well?'

'That's your next task,' Melville told him curtly. 'If we can find some ground for expelling von Huber from the country, both the Home Secretary and the President of the Board of Trade will be greatly indebted to us.'

'I appreciate the ironic use of "us",' Percy replied caustically, 'but may I take it that my fee will be guaranteed should I succeed, even though it hasn't yet been quantified?'

'Just get on with it, Enright!' Melville ordered as he half-rose from his seat.

'The name of this club in St James's, again?' Percy asked.

Melville consulted his notes. '"Montague's". Why, are you thinking of visiting it, even though you're not a member?'

'Not yet, admittedly,' Percy said with a slow smile. 'But then I'm not a member of Scotland Yard anymore, either. That doesn't stop me being called in when the establishment finds itself in trouble.'

'Is there *nothing* I can do?' Jack asked of Percy as they sat on the early evening train taking them back to Watford.

Percy thought for a moment, then nodded. 'You might want to take a little toddle down to the Tower and enquire further regarding Ponsonby's reputation down there, and the security of that armoury. Doesn't the Met have some general supervisory authority over Tower security?'

'Sort of,' Jack replied. 'It's never been fully explored, or pushed to the limit, but if, for example, someone were to be murdered within the Tower confines — a visitor, say, or one of the many domestic staff employed in there — then naturally we'd be called in. But if the matter's purely a military one, then the army tend to close ranks and tell us civilians to back off.'

'So if you make a big noise about the lost revolver being used to murder two civilians, which clearly *is* a Yard matter, you can insist on examining their records for something that Melville hasn't even thought through yet.'

'You'd really like to stick Melville's nose in it, wouldn't you?' Jack said with a smile.

'Well, there's something *else* he hasn't thought through, clearly,' Percy smirked. 'He insists that we can't be certain that the primary purpose of the double murder was to drop the prince in it. But if not, then why did Ponsonby go to considerable trouble to dump the gun on him?'

'Panic, perhaps, or a desire to point the finger away from himself,' Jack suggested.

'Perhaps,' Percy replied, 'but isn't it more exciting to think that we may hold the future direction of the British monarchy in our unworthy hands?'

CHAPTER ELEVEN

'I must confess that I've never heard of the "Home Office Gaming Club Inspectorate",' said Gilbert Drayton, secretary and manager of Montague's Club, 'but my very reliable doorman assures me that you're legitimate, so please tell me what I can do for you.'

The doorman in question had been the latest in a long line to be bamboozled by the card held high in the air for two seconds by Percy Enright — too high and too far away for the actual content to be read. The card was in fact an entry permit into the royal enclosure at the Royal Horticultural Society Great Spring Show of 1887, in which Percy's roses had been a prize-winner. He had kept it because of the impressive royal crest that was displayed at the top, which at a glance could be passed off as some sort of confirmation of office under the Crown.

'We're a fairly recent extension of the Lord Chancellor's theatre licensing function,' Percy replied smoothly, 'but inter-departmental rivalry led to my function being subsumed by the Home Office. This is probably the first time that you've been subjected to an inspectorial visit.'

'It most certainly is,' Drayton confirmed, 'but what is it that you need to know?'

Percy sat back with a reassuring smile, and he certainly looked the part for the role he was assuming. Dressed in his best three-piece suit, with a gold fob watch chain draped across his waistcoat, and with a pair of Beattie's spectacles hung around his neck — mainly because he wouldn't have been able to see a thing had he put them on — he oozed smoothly into the flattering mode that never failed to play on the interviewee's vanity.

'Since your club is so highly regarded, and so long established, we can dispense with the boring routine examination of all your relevant paperwork,' he announced, to an almost visible sigh of relief from Drayton. 'We can proceed to the most significant part of the duties that have been devolved upon me. As you'll appreciate, given your impressive membership list of the highest members of English society, the Home Secretary is anxious to ensure that no-one has acquired membership who might constitute a threat of some sort to the established order. Or, if they have, that you have appropriate procedures for weeding them out and terminating their membership.'

'Of course,' Drayton assured him. 'We are justifiably proud of the efforts we maintain to exclude those who are not, shall we say, the sort of person whose membership we would wish to encourage or tolerate.'

'Quite so,' Percy nodded. 'So you keep records of those whose membership has been terminated?'

'Of course,' Drayton assured him. 'We even keep a record of those whose membership has been temporarily suspended for some reason — perhaps an excusable oversight in the renewal of the annual subscription, or a failure to honour a debit account in the bar within the permitted time period.'

'This sounds excellent,' Percy said encouragingly, 'but I hope you will not be offended if I ask to see those lists, simply in order to certify to those who instruct me that I've inspected them.'

'Of course not,' Drayton replied as he rose, moved to a filing cabinet by the long window that looked out onto Green Park, and extracted a record book. Percy took it from him with an ingratiating smile, and opened it for long enough to confirm, with an inner sigh of contentment, that it was organised alphabetically. He kept his thumb on the index flag marked 'P', then suggested, 'Let's just take one or two at random, shall we? Purely for form, you understand?'

Ponsonby's name was certainly there, but a little subtlety was called for, so Percy selected another name and requested to be advised as to why one Algernon Palfreman had been expelled from the club the previous year.

Drayton's face took on a serious expression as he said, 'Unfortunately, Mr Palfreman's name appeared on a list of bad credit risks issued by a local private bank, and my trustees were firmly of the opinion that such a man was not the sort whose ongoing membership we should encourage. Mr Palfreman was quite understanding about it, and our judgment was vindicated when his name appeared in a bankruptcy notice only a few weeks ago.'

'An excellent exercise of discretionary judgment,' Percy confirmed. 'Do I take it from what you just told me that these decisions lie in the hands of a group of trustees?'

'Indeed,' Drayton confirmed, 'since this was the stipulation insisted on by Viscount Montague when he founded the club almost a century ago now. Clearly, to leave such sensitive matters in the hands of only one man such as myself would expose that person to unworthy temptation, so all significant matters involving our constitution and membership are referred to our trustees.'

'An excellent arrangement,' Percy agreed, 'and most commendable. I clearly need not take up much more of your valuable time, but I notice an entry here that puzzles me slightly. It seems to imply that a member was suspended for financial indebtedness, but then had his membership recently reinstated at the behest of the trustees.'

'Who was that?' Drayton asked.

Percy made a show of looking again at the name. 'Name of "Ponsonby",' he replied casually.

Drayton nodded. 'Oh yes, a most valued member. George Ponsonby, a Guards officer, and now personal valet to our new king. An excellent chap, and a regular at our baccarat table.'

'*Too* regular, it would seem from this,' Percy observed.

Drayton was eager to explain the circumstances more fully. 'That was most unfortunate, and I think that Captain Ponsonby has learned from his uncharacteristic impetuosity. Do you play baccarat at all?'

'Only occasionally, and never for high stakes,' Percy replied, maintaining his staid Government service persona.

'Well, as you'll know, it involves playing against a "banker", and the decision was made some time ago that in the best interests of both the club and its members, the bank in our baccarat games should remain in the hands of the croupier employed by the club. Anyway, although normally a player who enjoys both modest winnings and equally modest losses, Captain Ponsonby played one night after what may have been an inadvisable quantity of his favourite drink, which I believe is brandy. Whatever the reason, he found himself in considerable debt to the bank — a sum I believe to have approached several thousand pounds — and was unable to meet his obligations there and then. It's an invariable rule of the club that no member should bet beyond an amount that he can honour instantly, and so with regret we had to suspend his membership until the account was settled, which it was. That being the case, the trustees had no hesitation in reinstating his membership. So, as you can see, we are meticulous in upholding our house rules.'

'Yes, quite commendable,' Percy said ingratiatingly. 'How are these matters first brought to the attention of the trustees, might I ask?'

'They hold regular monthly meetings,' Drayton told him. 'Do you wish to see their minute book?'

'That would be most obliging of you, thank you,' Percy replied, and Drayton extracted the volume in question from a drawer in his desk. Percy had already made note of the date on which Ponsonby had been reinstated, which was only the previous December, and while making his perusal of the trustees' minute book appear casual, he flicked open the record for the monthly meeting held in the preceding November. Suppressing any sign of his mounting excitement, he asked, as casually as he could, 'Is it normal for one trustee to bring a matter to the attention of the remainder for discussion by them all?'

'Yes, that's their normal procedure,' Drayton replied. 'Is that a problem?'

'Indeed not,' Percy replied. 'It's just that I noticed that the reinstatement of Captain Ponsonby was proposed by one of the trustees — a man called Otto von Huber — and then voted on affirmatively by the remainder. This man, von Huber — is he, as his name suggests, a gentleman of German origin, and do you have no concerns about having a foreigner on your Board of Trustees?'

'Indeed not, in his case,' Drayton assured him. 'In fact, we are delighted to enjoy his membership, given that he's a highly respected industrial chemist, and approved of by his embassy to the extent that I believe he enjoys diplomatic immunity. We also number a French count and a minor Russian prince among our members.'

'Excellent,' Percy enthused as he made to rise from his seat in front of Drayton's desk. 'I don't really think I need to take up any more of your valuable time, and I may tell you, in the strictest confidence, of course, that my report on your club will be a most favourable one.'

'That's very gratifying.' Drayton beamed back at him as he reached for a form in a stack at the side of his desk. 'Here's a membership application form, should you feel sufficiently impressed by what you've learned today to wish to consider applying for membership.'

'I'll certainly be giving our conversation considerable thought,' Percy assured him as he allowed himself to be led back down the stairs to the entrance hall.

He couldn't resist a smirk as he walked back down St James's Street. 'Almost too easy,' he muttered as he caught the first horse bus of several that eventually conveyed him to his house in Hackney, which was currently empty because Beattie was still residing in Watford. After changing out of the suit he'd donned for the occasion into something more comfortable, he made his way to Euston Station with a light heart, anticipating being able to share with Jack, over supper, the considerable progress made in their enquiries.

Later that evening, Percy found it necessary to place his enthusiasm on hold when he entered The Lodge to find Jack in a state of outrage.

'Just look at this!' Jack shouted as he passed two sheets of paper to Percy the moment he entered the living room. 'Damned cheek, totally false, and deliberately misleading!'

Percy took the sheets and read them quickly in disbelief.

'It was served on me half an hour ago!' Jack added.

It was a summons for Jack to attend at the local magistrates' court in just over a week's time, charged under the Prevention of Cruelty to, and better Protection of, Children Act 1889. There were two charges on the summons, and when stripped of the non-essential verbiage, it was alleged that Jack had "on divers dates wilfully exposed a boy under the age of fourteen, to whit one Albert Enright, to unnecessary suffering or injury to his health."

Secondly, and during the same unspecified time frame, it was alleged that Jack had "caused a girl under sixteen years of age, to whit one Annabelle Pickering, to be in a circus to which the public were admitted by payment for the purpose of performing for profit."

'According to this, I could get three months!' Jack raged. 'And it's all a tissue of lies and twisted facts. It was the Earl of bloody Essex who was responsible for Bertie spraining his ankle when he fell off that rope, and Annabelle's stepfather who had her enticed away to the circus!'

'But somehow whoever made the complaint and swore out the summons had access to the basic facts in the first place, then twisted them into half-truths,' Percy pointed out. 'Has anyone been talking to the children lately, by any chance?'

'No idea,' Jack replied grumpily, 'because I haven't had a chance to speak to them yet. Esther insisted that they be allowed to have their meal before I tackled them on the subject.'

'I suggest that *we* do that now,' Percy replied as he turned and headed for the hallway. 'Are they in the kitchen?'

A minute later Percy and Jack stood just inside the kitchen door, with the children ranged down both sides of the long table, eating poached eggs on toast. As usual, alongside

Annabelle sat Beattie, armed with a book from which she was quietly reading for the girl's amusement, while Esther was pouring hot water from a pot into a teapot. She looked up with concern as she saw the two men enter the room.

'They haven't finished their tea yet,' she protested.

However, Jack was not in any mood to be dissuaded and asked, 'Have any of you — Annabelle and Bertie in particular — been speaking to strangers lately? When you went to the earl's house to return that gold cane, for example?'

'There was that funny little man who came up to us in the park,' Annabelle reminded Bertie, who sat across from her.

He nodded. 'But he wasn't anybody important — just a silly sort of person.'

'Did you talk to him?' Percy demanded as he looked intently at Annabelle, who seemed to shrink under his glare.

'You're frightening the girl by making her believe that she's done something wrong!' Beattie berated him, then she leaned down and said softly in Annabelle's ear, 'You're not in any sort of trouble, dear, but if you *have* been speaking to someone in the park, then Uncle Percy would like to know what was said.'

'Nothing, really,' Annabelle replied softly. 'We were coming back from the earl's house, and Bertie was limping on his new cane, and complaining that his ankle was hurting, when this funny little man came up to us and asked him why he was hobbling around like that, and Bertie told him.'

'What *exactly* did you tell him?' Jack demanded sharply, despite a warning glare from Esther.

'The truth,' Bertie insisted. 'I told him I'd been told to climb up a wall on a rope, and I'd slipped and fallen down, hurting my ankle.'

'Did you tell the man *which* wall?' Percy asked.

Bertie shook his head. 'No, he never asked. Then Annabelle told him that it had been all my fault because I hadn't been taught how to land properly, like she'd been taught in the circus.'

'You definitely mentioned the circus?' Jack asked.

'Yes,' Annabelle replied. 'I told him how my stepfather had let some people take me away to join the circus, but then I'd been rescued.'

'That explains everything,' Percy muttered in Jack's ear, then raised his voice again to ask the children, 'What did this man look like?'

'He was a funny little man, with red hair all over his face, except where there was a nasty scar under his eye,' Annabelle replied. 'And he talked funny and wasn't much taller than me.'

'Do you recognise that description?' Jack asked Percy, who nodded.

'I think so. Anyway, let's get down to the police station and quash this nonsense before it goes any further.'

An hour later they were standing at the public counter inside Watford Police Station, angrily confronting the sergeant behind it.

'This was served on me earlier today,' Jack snapped as he slammed the summons down on the counter, 'and it's all lies!'

'They all say that,' the sergeant replied wearily, 'but since you've been lawfully served, it'll be for the magistrates to decide the truth of it.'

'Is Inspector Bradbury still on duty, by any chance?' Percy asked as a possible shortcut suggested itself, and before Jack could strangle the sergeant.

'He's about to go off duty,' the sergeant told them, 'and he'll come down those stairs and through that door in a minute. Perhaps you should take a seat in the meantime.'

When the inspector duly appeared, in the process of putting on his top coat, Percy rose swiftly and intercepted him. 'Presumably you remember us?' he asked, as if there could be any doubt. 'We helped you solve that little matter of the abduction of a girl from Cassiobury House School, and assisted in the arrest of Alfred Pickering for the murder of his wife.'

'Yes, of course I remember,' the inspector replied wearily, 'but I'm just off home for the day.'

'Before you do that, you can right a serious wrong that's in danger of being inflicted on my nephew here,' Percy insisted. 'Chief Inspector Enright of Scotland Yard?'

'Yes, I remember you as well,' Bradbury confirmed as he paled slightly. 'What's the problem?'

'If you recall,' Jack began after taking a deep breath to calm himself, 'my wife is the deputy headmistress of the Cassiobury House School, and a girl was abducted from there and spirited away to a travelling circus that was in the area. A girl called Annabelle Pickering.'

'Yes. Wasn't it her stepfather who organised that — the man who subsequently murdered her mother?'

'Correct. Now some liar has alleged that I was the one who caused her to be in that circus, when it was myself and Mr Enright here who rescued her, with some help from the local bobbies.'

'Who's alleging that?' Bradbury asked.

Jack thrust the summons at him. 'Whoever laid the information on which *that* libellous allegation's based!' he insisted angrily.

Bradbury read it carefully, then nodded. 'There's obviously been a mistake here; I'll get that charge withdrawn. What about the first charge — is this "Albert Enright" your son?'

'Yes,' onfirmed, 'and he sprained his ankle falling off a rope he was climbing on the urging of the Earl of Essex, who will no doubt confirm that fact if you ask him. I had nothing to do with it, and in fact I've forbidden my son to have any more to do with that little boys' army that the earl seems to be recruiting.'

'That's not the first complaint I've had about that, so I'm prepared to take your word for it. Sergeant Miller?' he called, and the sergeant came out from behind his counter to be handed the summons by the inspector. 'Have this withdrawn immediately, on my authority.'

The sergeant nodded and returned behind his counter, while Bradbury turned back to address his two visitors. 'I can only apologise for what's happened. We were clearly given false information, and if there's anything further I can do…'

'You can reveal the identity of the person who *gave* you that false information,' Percy insisted.

Once again the sergeant was called out from behind his counter, carrying the papers that had been filed a few days earlier. He studied the papers for a moment, then announced, 'A Mr Hector Gillies, with an address in Islington.'

'I knew it!' Percy snarled.

'You know him?' Jack asked.

Percy nodded. 'I made his acquaintance not long ago, when a new client came to me complaining about his lack of action in return for an outrageous fee. And rest assured that I'll soon be renewing that acquaintance!'

CHAPTER TWELVE

Esther was waiting nervously for the return of Percy and Jack, and she met them in the hallway as they took off their coats and hung them on the stand by the front door.

'Well?' she asked.

Jack walked over to give her a reassuring hug. 'It's all resolved,' he told her. 'Percy knew precisely how to play that somewhat plodding inspector down there, and fortunately he remembered that we were the ones who rescued Annabelle from the circus. I also told him to enquire of the earl as to how Bertie came by that sprained ankle. He told the sergeant down there to cancel the summons.'

'But who would want to make such vile false allegations against us?' Esther asked. 'We simply offered Annabelle a home when she became an orphan. Why should someone wish to make us out to be bad parents?'

'I intend to discover that for myself tomorrow,' Percy announced. 'We know who it was who made those false complaints against Jack, and I believe that he was working for someone else.'

'You said that you know him,' Jack reminded him. 'How did that come about, and who is he?'

Percy gave a disapproving snort as he suggested that they move into the sitting room and refresh themselves with a drink before he enlightened them. A few minutes later, whisky and soda in hand, he explained, 'Hector Gillies is a private investigator of the worst sort — the type that gets "confidential enquiry agents" like me a bad name. You recall that Bertie and Annabelle reported that he had a scar just under one eye? Well, he got that in his hometown of Glasgow, and the knife that caused it was actually aimed at his eye. That gives you some idea of the sort of circles he moved in, which he moved out of very quickly and came south. He then set up a grubby little business above a surgical appliance shop in a far from salubrious street in Islington.'

'How do you know all this?' Esther asked.

'He tried to join an informal group of legitimate enquiry agents of which I'm a member. I'm proud to say that we sent him packing, but not before he'd given us his so-called business card. I dread to think what sort of clients he has, or what sort of business he attracts, but I'd be willing to bet that his attempt to blacken Jack's name was at the instigation of someone who's trying to set him up as a bad parent. Why precisely, I've no idea, but I suggest that Jack and I pay him a little visit tomorrow morning to find out.'

'Could it be connected with this Bradenham House enquiry that we're engaged on?' Jack asked.

Percy shook his head. 'I hardly think that the heir to the English throne would be hiring a man like Gillies.'

'Not him, obviously,' Jack replied, 'since we're working in his interests, as I understand it. But what about Ponsonby? If he suspects that we may be onto him, then he may be trying to ruin my reputation in advance. The investigation officially has my name on it, remember? Have you done or said anything lately to alert him to the fact that we may be onto him?'

'Funny you should mention that,' Percy said with a smile. 'In all the excitement of Jack being accused of child cruelty, I haven't had time to reveal my latest discovery. It leaves me in little doubt that Ponsonby had, and probably still has, an unhealthy connection with that German chap von Huber, who was the one who manoeuvred the prince into a compromising situation. That, in turn, makes me believe that that he was the real target, and not Belvedere. Von Huber simply cosied up to Belvedere in order to give Ponsonby an opportunity to make the prince look like a double murderer. Or perhaps just the murderer of Belvedere in the original plan, since I've come round to thinking that the other valet, Wilson, was done away with simply in order to allow Ponsonby to be on duty on the crucial evening.'

'So what's this link between Ponsonby and von Huber?' Esther asked.

'Gambling debts,' Percy replied. 'I believe that von Huber was playing what you might call a "long game", of which Ponsonby became the target once he became the prince's valet. Von Huber managed to get himself appointed as a trustee of Montague's, a club of which Ponsonby was an enthusiastic member and an addicted gambler at the baccarat table. One evening — and I'll wager that von Huber was somehow also behind this — Ponsonby wagered more than he was good for, and lost. He was unable to honour the debt on the spot, which under the club's rules required that he be suspended. Only weeks later he was able to repay the debt, *and* the person on the Board of Trustees who was instrumental in ensuring his reinstatement to membership was none other than von Huber. The coincidences are too strong to ignore. I suggest Ponsonby did what he did in order to have his gambling debts covered and his membership restored.'

'But what did this von Huber stand to gain by it all?' Esther asked.

'The suggestion from Melville of Special Branch is that von Huber was under instruction from Kaiser Wilhelm of Germany to prevent Prince Albert being crowned,' said Jack. 'The two have a mutual enmity that goes back years.'

Esther looked shocked as she replied, 'If that's the case, then the German Kaiser is attempting to interfere with the future of our nation. But if the issues are that important, and you're seeking to expose an international intrigue, then aren't both your lives in danger?'

Jack reached out to place a comforting hand on her shoulder. 'We've faced worse dangers in the past,' he reminded her.

Tears welled in her eyes. 'Yes, and they got you both shot. Is there no way you can back out of what you've taken on?'

'I wouldn't give Melville the satisfaction,' Percy said with a grin. 'And right now, the only danger we're in is of going to bed hungry. I take it that our supper's in the oven?'

'So apart from bearding this Gillies chap in his den,' Jack said to Percy the following morning as the eight-twenty from Watford rattled its way south through Harrow, 'what else do you propose that we do?'

'We should probably report my latest findings to Melville,' Percy replied. 'If you could set that up for some respectable hour this afternoon, we could savour a meat pie at Tang Li's.'

'Do your thoughts ever stray far from your stomach?'

'If you had a stomach the size of mine, would yours?' Percy chuckled. 'Anyway, when we confront Gillies, leave the talking to me.'

'I always do,' Jack smiled, 'but do you really need me there with you?'

'You're the aggrieved party,' Percy reminded him, 'and I need you to wear your "high-ranking Scotland Yard officer" hat. I have to admit that I'm rather looking forward to our little encounter. Let's just hope that he's in when we call at his office, although I doubt that he has many clients.'

The surgical appliance shop in Liverpool Road, Islington, appeared never to have received the attention of a window cleaner, as if embarrassed by the nature of the goods on sale inside. A handmade cardboard sign directed them down a rubbish-strewn side alley that smelt of tom cats, leading them to a peeling door that gave access to an unswept stone staircase. At the top of the staircase was another door that confirmed the presence within of one "Hector Gillies Esq, Private Investigator". Percy gently tested that door to confirm that it was not locked, then stood back and kicked it open.

The startled-looking man behind a rudimentary counter that also served as his desk fitted perfectly the physical description of him given by Annabelle following her encounter with him in Cassiobury Park. He was short and squat, with a face almost entirely obscured by a wild forest of red hair, and crawling up towards his right eye like a snake slithering out from undergrowth was a vivid red scar. He smiled uncertainly as he appeared to recognise Percy, and launched into a welcome.

'Good day to ye both,' he said. 'And what can I do for a fellow searcher after the truth?'

'I hope that your reference to "the truth" will prove to be something other than a figure of speech,' Percy all but shouted, 'otherwise you're about to be arrested for attempting to pervert the course of justice.'

'And what makes ye say that?' Gillies asked.

'The disgraceful and utterly unfounded allegations against a member of my family,' Percy replied coldly, 'or did the name "Enright" not ring a bell?'

'I know the name right enough,' Gillies said with a nod, 'but yours is "Percy" — is that not the case?'

Percy's eyes narrowed. 'Yes, it is, and the man you falsely accused is Jack Enright. You see this gentleman with me? *He's* the Jack Enright in question, and what you probably *didn't* know is that he's a Chief Inspector with Scotland Yard. You're under arrest for your lies.'

'Ah didnae know they were lies!' Gillies protested.

'Well, you know now,' Jack hissed as he held up his police badge. 'Hector Gillies, you're under arrest for…'

'Hey, hang on there a wee moment!' Gillies pleaded. 'Like I said, I didnae know that what I told the police in Watford was lies!'

'But you didn't bother checking what you'd been told, did you?' Percy thundered. 'And you want to be considered a private enquiry agent? You're a disgrace to the profession, and I'll make it my personal business to ensure that you never get another client unless you tell us who *that* one was. If you do, then my nephew here will know who to have charged.'

'Give me a minute,' Gillies requested as he reached into his desk, opened a drawer, fumbled around for a moment, then extracted a notebook. 'There ye go.' He smiled, revealing a dental graveyard. 'It was a lady in Cheltenham. Name o' Drinkwater — Rose Drinkwater. She told me she was after findin' a long-lost niece who had been kidnapped by your nephew there, and she was wantin' to get her back.'

Percy looked at Jack enquiringly. 'Does the name ring a bell?' he asked.

Jack shook his head. 'I seem to recall that Annabelle's mother had a sister in Cheltenham, who would of course be Annabelle's aunt, but beyond that I've no idea.'

'We'll make due enquiry,' Percy told Gillies. 'If what you tell us proves to be accurate, then you'll hear no more from us. But if these are more lies, pack your bags ahead of a lengthy spell in Newgate. Good day to you.'

As they walked back to the nearest horse bus stop, Jack asked, 'Why would Anabelle's aunt — if this Rose Drinkwater was indeed her — want to have me condemned as a bad parent?'

Percy thought hard. 'I can think of only one reason, Jack, and I suspect that you'll be hearing her name again. I only hope that you, Esther and Beattie have the fortitude to face what may be heading your way.'

Since it was not long before they could engage in a stroll down the Embankment to Tang Li's, Percy accompanied Jack as he went up to his office, checked his messages, then made arrangements for the two of them to meet with Melville in Bruce's office at three o'clock that afternoon. Then he went back to a message that seemed unfamiliar.

'Do we know a Sir Joseph Cranmer?' he asked Percy.

'No. With a name like that, he's hardly likely to be a casual acquaintance of either of us,' Percy replied. 'But it might have to do with the Belvedere matter. If you leave the message unanswered, he sounds like the sort of snotty aristocrat who could make Bruce's bowels knot themselves, so you'd better answer it while I compose the gist of what I'm going to tell Melville after we've fortified ourselves with meat pie.'

Jack dialled the number and found himself talking to a man who sounded like one of those who'd ushered them into the royal presence the previous week. 'Wait one moment, and I'll bring the master to the device,' he was instructed.

He waited for at least five minutes, then an even plummier voice dripped into his earpiece.

'Is that Chief Inspector Enright?' it asked, and when Jack confirmed that was the case, the man continued, 'I believe you're the man to have a chinwag with about that business at Bradenham House — have I got that right?'

'I'm certainly in charge of an investigation into a double death there a while ago,' Jack said, 'so how can I be of assistance?'

'It's the other way around, old boy,' he was told. 'If you could toddle down here sometime this morning, I can give you some useful information about what I saw, and perhaps put a stop to the beastly rumours that are flying around the head of a good friend of mine.'

'Does it have to be in person?' Jack asked. 'Can it not be done over the phone?'

'Don't trust these blessed things,' the man replied. 'The enemy has ears everywhere, we were always taught when I was in the Fifteenth Hussars. I'm not far away — Seventeen Cadogan Place, in darkest Belgravia. I'll be here until midday, then I'm off to Ascot. Tallyho and all that.'

The phone was put down with nothing further said, and Jack looked across at where Percy sat writing on a scrap of paper he'd scrounged from Jack's desk.

'That man reckoned he could tell me something about what happened at Bradenham House that weekend, and hinted that he'd be able to clear the name of a "good friend" of his,' he informed Percy.

'That sounds good,' Percy replied absentmindedly, 'so perhaps you'd better follow it up.'

'He wants me to go to his house in Belgravia before midday,' Jack added. 'That will delay our lunch.'

'That *doesn't* sound good,' Percy said, frowning as he suddenly paid attention, 'but I suppose duty comes before meat pie, so off you trot. Just grab what he can tell you, then beat a tactful retreat.'

The white-painted double oak doors were opened by a man resembling a pall bearer at a state funeral. He sniffed when Jack announced his identity, then glanced up and down the street of identical-looking Georgian mansions as if ashamed to be admitting a tradesman, albeit one of the law enforcement variety. Jack was hustled down a long, heavily carpeted and hideously wallpapered hall to a room at the end overlooking a park, where a cherub-faced man dressed in full morning attire rose to meet him. He gestured for Jack to take a hard-backed chair alongside the writing desk.

'Thank you for being so prompt,' the man said. 'I'm "Bugsy" Cranmer, and we spoke on that speaking tube.'

'Yes, indeed,' Jack confirmed, 'so what can you tell me about that double death in Bradenham House?'

'Is it true that Prince Albert is suspected of being involved?' Cranmer asked.

Jack shook his head. 'I'm not in a position to divulge details of our ongoing enquiries.'

'Quite. But can you tell me if you've put the finger on that obnoxious manservant of his — name of "Ponsonby"?'

'I presume that you're about to tell me why we should?'

'Absolutely,' Cranmer said with a nod. 'He was there when it happened, but the rat slunk out of there before anyone properly observed him. And he's a crack shot — with a shotgun, anyway.'

'You actually saw him there, while the bodies were lying on the floor?'

'Most certainly,' Cranmer confirmed. 'I was slightly at the back when we all rushed up there after hearing a couple of shots. I'm taller than most, so when they all crammed into the doorway, where our hostess was having a fit of the vapours, I could see over their heads, and Ponsonby was by Albert's bedside table. Then he slipped through a door that I assume led to the lavatory or something. He wasn't there when the police arrived, so to the best of my knowledge nobody asked him what he was about, and what he saw. And there's more.'

'Go on,' Jack urged him.

'Well, when I heard that someone had called in the police, I decided to take a walk out to the back of the house, for reasons we needn't explore further beyond the fact that I was the victim of a misunderstanding on the race track at Kempton Park a year or so back. Anyway, I saw the chap jumping off a sort of drainpipe on the back wall, then limping away like a horse with three legs. I thought it a bit of a dig in the circumstances, given that two dead men were staining the carpet in the room he'd just left. So you might want to shake him warmly by the throat and enquire as to what he saw and did. Just so that you know.'

'I'm greatly indebted to you,' Jack said with a smile, 'and it may well be that you'll be hearing from us again.'

'Only too glad to prove my bona fides to the guardians of the law,' Cranmer assured him, 'since it really *was* a misunderstanding about that bookkeeper chap at Kempton Park, and he made a swift recovery, or so I'm told.'

Jack could barely contain his excitement as he hurried down to Sloane Square, where he hailed a cab in order to return to Scotland Yard as quickly as possible. He had important news for Percy, and he was conscious that they might be late for lunch.

'That certainly adds a new arrow to our quiver,' Percy said forty minutes later as he fought down the disappointment of learning that the meat pie was finished for the day, and settled for lamb chops instead. Jack decided that he'd earned some sweet and sour pork as they considered their options and next move.

'We obviously have to tell Melville and Bruce what we've gleaned,' Percy said, 'and all we need to do now is demonstrate a clear connection between Ponsonby and this van Huber chap.'

'Surely that club of Ponsonby's is evidence enough?' Jack queried.

Percy shook his head. 'All that proves is that they knew each other, and perhaps, at a pinch, that they were friendly. Proving that von Huber put Ponsonby up to a double murder is another matter.'

'So how will you do that?' Jack asked.

'By employing sneaky tactics of which the Yard would not approve,' Percy said with satisfaction. 'That's why they called in my unique talents in the first place, remember? So finish your pork and let's go and touch our forelocks to our superiors, shall we?'

'You are strictly forbidden to blunder in against von Huber, do you understand?' Melville told Percy sharply as he revealed the latest discoveries in their investigations.

'I hear what you say,' Percy insisted, 'but if we're right, and von Huber's in cahoots with Ponsonby, we need to flush the pair of them out somehow.'

'You can't be sure that they are,' Melville countered, 'and the last thing we need right now is a diplomatic row with Germany. Von Huber's a respected member of our commercial community, as well as Germany's, and I'm advised by the Board of Trade that we need to keep our options open regarding his advanced steelmaking knowledge.'

'We also need to dig Prince Albert out of trouble,' Percy fired back, 'which is the task you gave to us — not one of maintaining a friendly relationship with the Germans.'

Melville blanched, then turned to Bruce. 'If Enright goes anywhere near von Huber, I'll hold you responsible, understood?'

Bruce bridled as he replied, 'You're the one who wanted to unleash a mad dog into the picture — now you want *me* to be responsible for who he bites?'

'Just don't let him loose anywhere near von Huber, that's all,' Melville snarled as he rose to leave.

When Percy and Jack returned to Jack's office a few minutes later, Jack asked, 'What do we do now? Our hands are tied behind our backs.'

'Our hands, certainly,' Percy said, 'but not our mouths. And that's what mad dogs employ as weapons. Do you have any friends in the Board of Trade?'

CHAPTER THIRTEEN

'Why should we fear anything from this Rose Drinkwater?' Jack asked as he and Percy sat side by side on the train home. 'If she *is* Annabelle's aunt, then surely she should be happy that her niece has a secure and happy home life with us, rather than being consigned to an orphanage by the authorities?'

'We don't know for certain that she is Annabelle's aunt,' Percy replied, 'although when we get back to Watford, we can of course ask her. But if she is, ask yourself what motive she might have for setting out to prove that you and Esther are not fit guardians of her niece.'

'In order to remove her from our care, obviously, but that would surely result in Annabelle being adjudged an orphan?'

'Not for as long as she has a living relative prepared to take her in. Think it through, Jack.'

'You mean she intends to step in and take Annabelle to live with her? Can she do that? And, more to the point, *why* would she do that?'

'As for why, perhaps she's childless and feels an aching emptiness in her life — your Aunt Beattie could tell you all about that, believe me. And I can tell you from professional experience that the "how" is by means of a court action.'

'So you're a lawyer now as well, is that it?' Jack said grumpily.

'Obviously not, but I've done enquiry work for a few, and one in particular. His name is Spencer Launceston, and he's a barrister with chambers in Lincoln's Inn. He specialises in all sorts of legal work involving families, and more than once he's hired me to enquire into the circumstances in which children are living, usually when one of the parents, following a divorce, is seeking custody of a child of the marriage. It's a fairly straightforward process in the Court of Chancery in The Strand, and occasionally I've been called to give evidence regarding the conditions in which I found a child living.'

'And you think that Esther and I might become entangled in something like that?'

'It's possible, but as I already cautioned you, we don't know who this "Rose Drinkwater" is. But Annabelle can clearly confirm whether or not she's her aunt.'

Once they'd reached The Lodge and removed their coats, they walked into the sitting room, where the children were seated as close to the roaring fire as Esther would permit, each engaged in their own chosen activity. Bertie as usual was arranging his soldiers on the carpet in preparation for a combined attack on the underside of the sideboard, Lily was sewing something or other, Miriam and Tommy were playing some sort of card game, and Annabelle was reading out loud from a novel while Beattie smiled her encouragement, one arm draped around the girl's shoulders. Esther was seated by the fire, repairing Bertie's school trousers yet again.

'Annabelle,' Jack asked, 'do you know a lady called Rose Drinkwater?'

'She's busy reading,' Beattie said with a warning frown, 'and she's acquitting herself very well indeed, so don't interrupt.'

'She's my aunt,' Annabelle said with a pout, 'and I don't like her.'

'Why not?' Jack persevered.

'She's very strict, and very — well, "formal", I suppose. Her husband — my Uncle Thomas — is a lawyer, and he's hoping to become the Mayor of Cheltenham one day, so they're always having dinner parties and things. Mama used to send me to stay with them sometimes, and I always had to behave like a little lady whenever they had company. Sometimes I was allowed to be in the room, when they asked me to sing some awful song while Aunt Rose played the piano, but most of the time I was sent to my room and told not to make a noise.'

'So you didn't enjoy your visits to Cheltenham?' Percy asked, receiving a hard glare from Beattie.

'No,' Annabelle replied, 'I used to hate them. I would beg Mama not to send me there again, but sometimes she and my stepfather wanted to take a holiday somewhere, and my stepfather never wanted me around when they did, so I was sent to Cheltenham.'

'So you wouldn't want to live with your aunt?' Jack asked.

Annabelle's face crumpled, warning of impending tears as she blurted out, 'You're going to send me there, aren't you? I thought I could live *here*, and I've done my best to be good. I don't eat much, and I always make my bed and help Lily tidy our room — *please* don't send me away!'

'What on earth's got into you two?' Beattie demanded angrily as she placed another protective arm around a now sniffling Annabelle and hugged her. 'Are you trying to frighten the poor child? And if so, why? What has her aunt got to do with anything?'

'Beattie has a good point,' Esther added as she looked up sternly from her sewing. 'But you must have some reason for these questions. Has the woman written to us, asking for Annabelle to be sent to her? If so, why did you keep that letter from me?'

'She was the one behind all those lies about our alleged cruelty towards the children,' Jack replied. 'Percy and I tracked down that grubby little man who Bertie and Annabelle met in the park. He's the lowest sort of so-called "private investigator", and was hired by Rose Drinkwater to find evidence that we weren't fit to be looking after Annabelle.'

'But he failed,' Esther reminded him, 'so why are we still talking about it?'

Jack looked meaningfully at Percy, who explained, 'I believe that this Rose Drinkwater may be contemplating bringing a court action to gain custody of Annabelle, so be prepared to receive court papers at some time in the future.'

'Don't let her!' Annabelle wailed. '*Please* don't let her! I'd rather die than go and live with her. I'm *so* happy here with Lily and everyone else. If you let her get me, I'll run off to the circus again, I *swear* I will!'

'That's *enough*!' Beattie shouted as she lifted Annabelle to her feet and pulled her gently towards the hall door. 'The poor girl's terrified — can't you see that? You've done enough damage for one day — now leave her alone!'

It fell briefly silent as Beattie helped a sobbing Annabelle towards the staircase, promising to bring her a cup of hot chocolate and her favourite eggs on toast for her tea. The remaining children looked either shocked or embarrassed, and Lily offered to go and keep Annabelle company in their room.

'Leave that to Aunt Beattie, dear,' Esther instructed her, then turned to Jack and Percy. 'Beattie had a point, and I agree with her. You had no business frightening Annabelle like that. I hope you're both ashamed of yourselves, and I can only hope that Percy can deal with the problem when, and if, it arises. But from now on I'll be very apprehensive when I see the postman arriving.'

'Court papers don't arrive by post,' Percy told her. 'They're "served" on you by an officer appointed by the court. I did that sort of work myself for a while, when I was just getting started as an enquiry agent.'

'Well, I can only hope that you can bring your devious talents to our assistance when and if we get "served",' Esther insisted. 'After all, there has to be *some* advantage in having you around, and it'll make up for frightening Annabelle like that. I'm sure that Beattie will give you a piece of her mind at bedtime, so I'll leave it at that.'

As it transpired, they only had one night to wait before the blow fell. Esther came home the following afternoon from her working day at Cassiobury House School, with Lily and Annabelle deep in conversation a few paces behind her, to find a shabby-looking man waiting inside their front gate.

'Mrs Enright?' he asked, and Esther confirmed her identity with a sinking feeling, nervously aware of the bundle of papers he was holding. 'These are for you,' he went on brusquely as he held them out, and when Esther seemed reluctant to take them from him, he smiled unpleasantly and laid them on the gravel drive in front of her. 'Whether you like it or not,' he told her solemnly, 'you've been lawfully served, and my job is done.'

He walked away, leaving a trembling Esther to pick up the papers and glance apprehensively at the top page. She read as far as "Court of Chancery", then shuddered and ushered the two girls into the house. Two hours later, when Jack and Percy returned, she was seated alone in the dining room, the papers spread out before her on the table, with tears rolling down her face.

'It's happened just like you said,' she choked as she looked up at Percy. 'It looks as if that dreadful aunt of Annabelle's has done precisely what you predicted, and we have to go to court in order to keep dear little Annabelle as part of the family. You're the one with all the appropriate ideas for situations like this — what can we possibly do? We obviously aren't lawyers, and if Annabelle's taken from us, I'll simply *die*!'

She finally gave way to heartrending sobs, and Percy looked at Jack.

'Comfort Esther while I make use of that telephone that the Met installed for the betterment of your duties. Hopefully the man's still in his chambers, and prepared to do something for me for a change.'

Esther had more or less composed herself by the time he returned and told them, 'I took the liberty of inviting Spencer Launceston to visit us all for lunch on Saturday. That's an achievement in itself, given his busy schedule, the short notice, and the fact that he normally enjoys fishing trips off Southend at the weekends. So "be of good cheer", as the old saying goes, and let's wait until we learn what he can tell us before we let our spirits sink. The man's the best at what he does, and we have to be at *our* best when we meet with him. Now, would it be callous and inappropriate of me to enquire what's for dinner?'

By Saturday morning the house was as immaculate as scrubbing by an exhausted Alice could make it, and a delicious aroma of roast beef was wafting from the kitchen into the hallway as Percy introduced Spencer Launceston to Jack. Their visitor looked every inch the experienced, suave and confident barrister at law as he shook Jack's hand warmly.

'Percy's already told me a lot about you and your family,' said the lawyer, 'but I wanted to begin my representation of you by meeting you all. That way, I can get some ideas regarding how to frame my court strategy.'

'Yes, of course,' Jack said with a smile as he waved a hand towards the sitting room door. 'They're all in there, and anxious to meet you.'

They all looked up expectantly as Jack, Percy and Launceston joined them.

'Well, it certainly *looks* like a happy family, so I need to begin by learning all your names,' said Launceston. 'This delightful lady I take to be Mrs Enright, and the older lady to perhaps be her mother?'

Beattie gave a slight snort as she told him, 'I'm another Mrs Enright, certainly, but not Esther's mother. Percy, who you've already met, is my husband, and I'm Jack's aunt.'

'My apologies,' Launceston smiled graciously, 'but from the little that Percy's told me already, I gather that you've taken a special interest in the girl at the centre of the matter that I'm being briefed in. Which of you young ladies is Annabelle?'

'That's me,' Annabelle told him in a small voice, 'and I don't want to be sent to live with my aunt!'

'Hopefully you won't be,' Launceston replied reassuringly, 'but who are all these other young people?'

'I'm Lily, Annabelle's best friend,' Lily piped up, 'and *I* don't want her to leave here either.'

'I'm Bertie,' Albert added. 'I'm really called Albert, but everyone just calls me Bertie, and I want to be a soldier one day.'

'I'm Miriam,' squeaked the smallest of the girls. 'I'll be six years old soon, and I like playing with my dollies. This is my little brother Tommy, and I can climb trees faster than he can.'

'So you have these four children, as well as having taken over responsibility for young Annabelle?' Launceston asked by way of clarification. 'This is obviously a substantial house, but do you have enough room for them all?'

'Lily and Annabelle are good friends, as you've already been told,' Esther replied with a warm smile, 'and they share a bedroom. Annabelle's fitted in *so* well, and you wouldn't believe what a sad, downtrodden little girl she was when she first came to live with us. I'm her schoolteacher as well as her substitute mother, and I've seen the most encouraging development in her since she was first in my class. She used to be too timid to say anything because of the way her stepfather at that time constantly belittled her.'

'*He* was hanged, of course,' Beattie reminded them all bluntly, 'after he murdered her mother. *Quite* the wrong environment for a child to be raised in, but with God's great mercy and love she's found a home here, and she can already read books that I would have considered only appropriate for an educated adult. If you deem this house to be too crowded already, then Percy and I have our own substantial house in Hackney. Percy's retired from his career in the Metropolitan Police, of course, and has begun a new career, but we'd both be more than happy to take Annabelle into our home. We're childless, you see.'

'Everyone seems to be forming a polite queue to give you a new home, Annabelle,' Launceston said, smiling down at her, 'but what do *you* want?'

'I want to stay here!' Annabelle insisted. 'I've stayed with Aunt Rose on holidays, and she's *horrid*! If I get sent to live with her, I'll escape and join the circus!'

'Well, let's hope that doesn't happen, shall we?' Launceston replied warmly, just as Alice poked her head round the sitting room door.

'Polly says that lunch will be on the table in ten minutes, and will the children be eating in the kitchen as usual?' she asked.

'Yes, please,' Esther replied, 'since we need to speak with Mr Launceston over lunch.' Then she turned to address the children. 'Time to wash your hands before lunch, children, then go into the kitchen, where Polly's cooked sausages specially for you.'

When the adults were seated around the table, Launceston smiled and nodded for Alice to serve him a third slice of beef. 'You seem a very happy family,' he observed, 'and this is far better than the bread and cheese that I normally eat for my lunch on Saturday, when I cast my line over the side of the boat while gazing up at the end of Southend Pier.'

'It's very good of you to give up your day just for us,' Jack murmured appreciatively.

'It's also very good of *you* to share your happy home with me, if only for the day,' said Launceston. 'In my line of work, I spend so much time exposed to unhappy families, as you'll appreciate, and it falls to Percy here to provide me with all the depressing details. For once he's provided me with a warm experience, and one that I can make great use of once we get to court.'

'I must confess my ignorance of these matters,' Esther said. 'I thought that it was only possible to apply for custody of a child if one was a parent — for example, during or following divorce proceedings. I have a child in my class who's been claimed by his father, after it was proved that his mother had formed a new relationship, and was living with a man who earns his living by receiving property stolen by others.'

'This is perhaps not the best time for me to give you a legal lecture,' Launceston began, 'but I can answer that question easily, and it's relevant to the challenge that you're all facing. For almost thirty years now, child custody has been governed by an Act of Parliament that allows close relatives other than a mother to seek custody of a child. In this case, of course, the child's aunt. But — and this is a *very* important "but" — that same legislation also places the welfare of the child at the forefront of those factors that the judge has to consider. In one sense, of course, it gives the judge in question the power of Almighty God, but in another it allows him to take into account the wishes of the child, and Annabelle has left me in no doubt of where she's happy to remain, and where she *doesn't* want to go.'

'Did I understand you to say that only "close relatives" can apply for custody under this legislation?' Beattie chipped in. 'Clearly, none of us is blood related to Annabelle, so won't that go against us?'

Launceston shook his head. 'It obviously would, were you the ones applying for custody, but you're not. The ultimate question for the judge will be whether or not it's in Annabelle's best interests to go and live with her aunt. If he can be satisfied, on a "balance of probabilities", as we lawyers say, that it's in her best interest to remain where she is, then he'll simply reject her aunt's application.'

'Can't we simply apply to become Annabelle's new parents?' Jack asked.

'There's currently no law that permits such an application, but if the judge is satisfied that Annabelle is better off where she is, then in effect you *will* become her parents.'

'And if she came to live with us, then *we'd* become her parents in the eyes of the law?' Beattie asked with a gleam in her eye.

'Yes, I suppose so, in a sense,' Launceston conceded, 'and you've just given me another line of thought. Annabelle goes to school here in Watford, does she not, so it's convenient for her to be living here during the school term?'

'Yes, that's right,' Esther confirmed, 'and as I already told you, her progress at school has improved remarkably since she's been living with us.'

'But what about during the school holidays?' Launceston asked.

'We were already talking about her spending her school holidays with us in Hackney,' Beattie replied eagerly. 'We have more than one spare room, and Jack here spent five years living with us when his father died. I think you'll agree that he came to no harm in the process.'

'Quite,' Launceston replied thoughtfully. 'So if I were to propose that Annabelle be allowed to live here during school terms, and stay with you during her holidays, you'd be agreeable?'

'We'd be *overjoyed!*' Beattie enthused. 'Would the judge agree to that?'

'We can only ask,' Launceston said with a shrug.

It was mid afternoon before Launceston left, with handshakes all round, and a kiss on the cheek from Annabelle when, at her request, Beattie lifted her off the ground for that purpose. As they turned back from waving Launceston off in his hired coach, Beattie turned to Percy.

'I don't know what you were thinking of doing next week, Percy Enright, but take it from me that you'll be preparing our house for the next school holidays, which are only a month away.'

CHAPTER FOURTEEN

The Board of Trade had proved very helpful, although unaware that they were assisting Percy to circumvent a direct order from the head of Special Branch. Shortly after eleven o'clock on a bright spring Monday morning, a smartly dressed private secretary to Otto von Huber showed "Mr Percival" into von Huber's spacious office on the second floor of a prestigious office block in Dorset Street, Marylebone.

'My secretary did not mention why you wish to see me,' von Huber smiled as he waved Percy into the plush visitor's chair, and sat back in his own behind a desk resplendent with gold ink stands and brass candle holders.

'That's because he didn't ask,' Percy replied solemnly. 'If he had, I would have been obliged to tell a lie, since were the purpose of my visit to have been disclosed in advance, you would not have agreed to see me.'

'Before you embark on some sort of threat,' von Huber replied in immaculate English that bore only the trace of an accent, 'you should be aware that I am accredited with the German Embassy in Carlton House Terrace, and that I enjoy diplomatic immunity.'

'Oh, I was well aware of that,' Percy said confidently, 'and I am also well aware that should I attempt to have you prosecuted for your part in a double murder, you'd call in the German establishment and have yourself whisked back to your homeland under the cover of darkness. I am here merely to deliver a message to your partner in crime.'

Von Huber allowed himself a cold laugh. 'To what do you refer in your obvious delusion?' he asked.

'The murder of Sir Rupert Belvedere and his valet, James Wilson, during a hunting party weekend at Bradenham House in Buckinghamshire, at which you were an invited guest, along with the then Prince Albert, shortly to become King Edward the Seventh of England, unless that has been prevented by your cleverly worked scheme.'

'I was present at that weekend gathering, certainly,' von Huber agreed, 'as the guest of Sir Rupert, for whom I was acting as a technical consultant for his steel enterprise.'

'That was your cover,' Percy continued, undaunted, 'but it gave you the perfect opportunity to contrive a situation in which your accomplice could murder two men and allow the suspicion for those murders to fall upon Prince Albert.'

'Who is this so-called "accomplice", and what exactly do you allege was my part in what happened?' von Huber asked haughtily. 'You were not there at the time, whereas I was, and I clearly saw with my own eyes the facts that left no possible doubt that Prince Albert had shot two men dead.'

'Thank you for at least conceding that you were there,' Percy smiled, 'but it might have been more forthcoming had you admitted that you were the one who manipulated the situation so that the prince was persuaded to retire to his bedchamber and place a blindfold over his eyes while your accomplice shot Sir Rupert. He had already disposed of the valet Wilson, and dragged his body into the bedchamber from where he'd hidden it in the adjoining dressing room.'

'Again you fail to name my alleged accomplice,' von Huber replied confidently.

'Walter Ponsonby, the prince's own personal valet,' Percy said, raising his eyebrows.

Von Huber's expression didn't change. 'I was obviously aware that the man had accompanied the prince to Bradenham

House, but so far as I recall he'd been given the day off to take part in the hunt, where he acquitted himself well. But that was the first time I'd ever laid eyes on him, to the best of my knowledge.'

'Then it was strange indeed,' Percy countered, 'that this was the same man whose reinstatement to membership of Montague's, of which you are a trustee, you had personally proposed. Do you normally perform such services for men you've never met? And what became of his gambling debt? Perhaps you were the one who paid it off?'

'You claim to be well informed,' von Huber said with a smirk, 'but what goes on inside Montague's is a matter between its members and the trustees, surely?'

'Unless one speaks to its secretary and manager, a most obliging Mr Gilbert Drayton,' Percy replied. 'You must admit that all the circumstances suggest that you recruited Mr Ponsonby to kill two men in order to make Prince Albert look like a double murderer, at the bidding of your friends in the German Embassy. And before you remind me once again of your diplomatic immunity, let me assure you that the purpose of my visit here today is not to bring about your arrest, nor even to seek money for my silence — not from you, anyway.'

'Then why are you here?'

'I wish you to contact Mr Ponsonby — and please don't waste any more of our valuable time by insisting that you don't know him. Just tell him that ten thousand pounds will secure my silence, and that it may be delivered to my home at eight o'clock on Wednesday evening. I want high-denomination banknotes, since they are easier to count. The address is number thirty-seven, Victoria Park Road, Hackney, and I will ensure that I am alone in the house when Mr Ponsonby calls. Is there any other information you require?'

'Yes,' von Huber said with a glare. 'What if this Mr Ponsonby does not present himself as requested, since I have no idea where I might find him?'

'You'll find him in attendance on Prince Albert, no doubt, or perhaps at Montague's. But if you do not, or if for some other reason he does not avail himself of this wonderful opportunity to keep *both* of your names out of this business, then *he'll* be for the hangman, and you'll no doubt be deported. I'll show myself out.'

'Why do you have such a long face?' Jack asked as they sat across from each other at Tang Li's following Percy's meeting with von Huber.

Percy put down his knife and fork — a rare action for him, and a good indication that he had something important to say. He looked Jack squarely in the eye.

'Are you prepared to take a huge risk in order to bring this latest investigation to a successful conclusion?'

'Of course,' Jack reassured him, 'but why do you need to ask?'

Percy sighed. 'It's just that I'm beginning to feel like a one-man operation. I've taken steps to complete this strange task dumped on us by Special Branch to enable our new king to be crowned, and at the very last minute Melville refuses to lend us the manpower. I'm going to have to be very inventive and take a huge gamble. If it pays off, we won't need any more trips into Buckinghamshire, but if it doesn't I'll either be dead or in prison for a very long time into my retirement.'

'You're being even more obtuse than normal,' Jack complained. 'Just tell me what you need me to do.'

'In due course,' Percy replied, 'I wish you to meet someone very important to the joint enquiries on which we've embarked, but prior to that I need you to assist with the task that Beattie set me of preparing the house for the arrival of our pretend daughter Annabelle.'

'That goes without saying,' Jack assured him, 'since it was the house that was so welcoming to me all those years ago. But I'm no good at cleaning, as Esther can tell you. On the contrary, I'm frequently accused of making the messes in the first place.'

'I shall of course be employing cleaners,' Percy said with a frown, 'but I need your expert eye as a father, and a former resident of the house, to ensure that it's as welcoming as possible. The Easter school holidays are almost upon us, and by the time we get to court Annabelle will have spent her first holiday with us. If she doesn't report back favourably on that, my life won't be worth living.'

'But I have my work up the road to catch up on,' Jack pointed out, 'while you no doubt have clients clamouring for your services during the days. Are you proposing that we somehow set about this task by night?'

'On evenings only,' Percy assured him, 'although that will clearly require us both to take up residence in the house, making use of a local eatery for our evening meals. I intend to carry out fairly substantial amendments to the facilities by day, and rely on your comments when you return here for your evening meal.'

'And what about our work on the Bradenham House double murder enquiry?'

'That should resolve itself when we play host to a visitor on Wednesday evening. So, are you up for it?'

'Of course, but what do we tell Esther and Beattie?'

'The truth, for once. I'll make a telephone call to Beattie at The Lodge, and tell her what we have in mind. You might wish to have Esther send you down a change of clothes, which I'll instruct Jennings to collect for you, and have them waiting for you in Hackney. It'll be like old times, apart from Beattie's cooking.'

On the Monday evening Jack was both surprised and delighted to discover that his old room in the house on Victoria Park Road had become one more suited to a girl approaching ten years of age, with a desk and chair beneath a magnificent painting of a mountain range, as well as fresh curtains that depicted scenes from fairy stories. He had no objection to sleeping on a spare bed in the kitchen, and even less objection to taking his evening meal in the rear room of The Mermaid in Mare Street, only a short walk from the house.

When he returned on the Tuesday evening, the front garden had been transformed. Gone were the dead bushes that had lined the uneven path; now there was a new concrete walkway still drying in the early evening sunlight, with rows of firs in plant pots on either side of it. Jack was obliged to make use of the back door down the side alley between Percy's house and the one next door, but he was assured that the front path would soon be ready for use.

'I've decided against visiting The Mermaid today,' Percy announced the following evening, a Wednesday, as he and Jack sat in the kitchen. 'Instead I thought I'd nip down to the cook shop a few doors further up Mare Street and bring us back something to share with the visitor we'll be entertaining this evening. Perhaps a load of lamb chops with all the vegetables.'

'Sounds good,' Jack agreed, 'but what time are you expecting this guest, and who is he — or she?'

'You'll find out soon enough, but in the meantime indulge me in another of my guessing games,' Percy said with a smile. 'I'll head off now, but if he arrives while I'm out, just show him in and give him a drink to await my return.'

At precisely eight o'clock there was a heavy knock on the front door, and Jack put down his whisky glass and went into the hall to answer it. There was a light above the front door that Jack had no memory of ever noticing before, and in its glow stood a tall man of approximately the same age as Jack, but with close-cropped fair hair and a droopy ginger moustache that was the height of fashion.

'Mr Enright?' the man asked as he reached inside his jacket pocket.

'Which one were you seeking?' Jack asked, and in an instant there was a hurried movement from between the two ornamental firs closest to the door, and a gun appeared on the end of Percy's hand, its barrel pressed firmly against the back of the man's head. There was an ominous click as the hammer was pulled back prior to firing, and Percy's cold voice seemed to echo around the narrow doorway.

'It was *this* one he was seeking, but I anticipated his arrival. If the other Mr Enright would be so good as to investigate the inside of our visitor's jacket, I think he'll find one of those weapons missing from the Tower Armoury. In the meantime, I'll call in some reinforcements.'

Jack foraged in the man's inside jacket pocket and relieved him of a five-barrelled Webley revolver, while Percy extracted a police whistle from his waistcoat pocket and blew three shrill blasts on it. The driveway seemed to fill with blue serge uniforms, and Percy gave a loud chuckle.

'I opted for the local force when Melville proved so reluctant to supply men of his own. I am still fondly remembered from my days as a sergeant here, when some of these fine fellows were beginning their recruit training. Very well, gentlemen, I yield into your custody a man named Walter Ponsonby. Chief Inspector Enright, who's the man in the doorway doing impersonations of a startled deer, will advise you of the charges, since it's his arrest.'

'A double murder, and the theft of this revolver that I've just taken from his jacket,' Jack announced. 'Make sure that you lock him up securely, and we'll no doubt be renewing our acquaintance with him in the morning.'

The men led Ponsonby down the driveway to a waiting coach that had just pulled up in the road, driven by Jennings.

Percy turned back to grin at Jack. 'Sorry about that, Jack my boy, but "needs must", as someone once said.'

'I could have been killed!' Jack protested as his heart resumed beating at its customary pace.

'Trust me, no-one would have regretted that more than me — except perhaps yourself. But do you have any questions?'

'Yes,' Jack replied. 'What did you get for our supper?'

CHAPTER FIFTEEN

'Three sausages or four?' Percy asked as he looked down at where Jack lay in his makeshift bed, slowly coming awake to the entrancing smell of breakfast being prepared a few feet above him.

'Make that six,' Jack replied, 'since you deprived me of any supper. I'll go to relieve myself, then I'll set the table, and you can tell me why you risked me getting shot.'

Ten minutes later, both men were seated at the table.

'There was no real risk of Ponsonby getting off a shot at you,' Percy assured him as he slid the second fried egg onto Jack's plate ten minutes later.

'You took a huge gamble,' Jack complained. 'Apart from anything else, if he'd shot me, then you, he'd have escaped from the only two who could point the finger at him. Melville would never have put the pieces together the way we did.'

'The way *I* did, you mean,' Percy grunted. 'And we can still only charge him with stealing those revolvers from the Tower Armoury, unless we get a confession.'

'Which we'll presumably set about this morning?'

'Perhaps, and perhaps not,' Percy replied. 'The holding cell — which is the *only* cell — inside Hackney Police Station is very unpleasant at the best of times, and is made even less habitable by the number of drunks, prostitutes and vagrants that you have to share it with. After a couple of days in there, he'll probably be willing to peach on his own mother.'

'The Procedures Manual says that we have to bring him before a magistrate without undue delay,' Jack reminded him.

'It was my capacity for stepping around the Procedures Manual, with deft footwork worthy of a ballet dancer, that induced Melville to employ me in this case,' Percy retorted. 'One of the factors that persuaded me to accede to his plea for help was the mortal blow that such a decision must have dealt to his insufferable pride. We are officially still pursuing the evidence in this case, you will recall. The Procedures Manual makes provision for a man to be held in custody if there is an "appreciable danger" that by releasing him he'll be at risk of interfering with that evidence in some way. Such as, in this case, alerting von Huber to his plight, and allowing him to pull diplomatic strings.'

'So how long do you intend to leave Ponsonby languishing in a smelly cell in a provincial lock-up?'

'Until we've availed ourselves of a splendid lunch at The Mermaid, with the smell of it lingering on our clothes when we go in to enquire how he enjoyed a mug of weak tea and a slice of bread spread thinly with jam.'

Shortly before three o'clock that afternoon a sour-faced Ponsonby, suitably secured at the wrists and ankles, was led into the small room in Hackney Police Station that was reserved for interviews with both suspects and witnesses. Percy allowed himself a grim smile.

'It's customary at this point for me to enquire as to whether or not you've been well treated while here as our guest. But I won't ask you, because I don't think I could bear the disappointment if you tell me that you *have* been.'

'Just get on with it,' Ponsonby growled. 'You're not even a police officer anymore, are you?'

'I wonder who told you that — von Huber, presumably?' Percy asked. 'But while I may no longer be an officer of the

Metropolitan Police, the man seated beside me — the man who you mistook for me — is a chief inspector, and this interview is officially being conducted by him. But it might be to your advantage if you continue to converse with me.'

'You're going to pretend to offer me a deal, I assume?' Ponsonby snapped.

'Well, look at it this way: the task we were set was not to prove you guilty of two murders. It was, in fact, to prove that someone *else* wasn't.'

'You refer to my master the prince?'

'Your *former* master, I think you'll find, after you're charged with the theft of several revolvers from the Tower Armoury.'

'So you're out to prove that he didn't fire those shots? Well, what's in it for me if I assist in that?'

'The gratitude of your former master, obviously. And he has considerable leverage in these matters. A brief word from him to the Home Secretary might well reduce the charges you're facing. All we need you to confirm is that it was not Prince Albert who fired those shots.'

'And if I don't cooperate?'

'I think you know the answer to that question,' Percy replied solemnly. 'Newgate, a trial, a certain finding of guilt on the evidence we've already acquired, then the long drop.'

'If I were to admit to committing these two murders, then the outcome would be the same, of course, so I ask again — what's in it for me?'

'If you're prepared to admit to the shootings in circumstances that might open the door to an agreed plea of "guilty of manslaughter", then the outcome would obviously be a prison sentence but no hanging. And the length of that sentence might well be substantially influenced by a supportive letter from the Home Secretary.'

'And you have him in your pocket, no doubt,' Ponsonby replied sarcastically.

'*I* don't, of course,' Percy conceded, 'but who can foresee what a grateful king might be capable of? All the ministers under the Crown are susceptible to influence from the palace.'

Ponsonby fell silent, then asked, 'What sort of "circumstances" had you in mind, given the facts?'

'I'm renowned for my powers of invention,' Percy assured him, 'as the chief inspector here can confirm. By the way, and for the record, he's also my nephew.'

'You set him up to be shot?' Ponsonby asked in disbelief. 'You must be very desperate to get Prince Albert off the hook.'

'Everyone in government is,' said Percy, 'and your assistance in that would be gratefully received. *Very* gratefully, I might add. How does a five-year stretch appeal to you?'

'You can make that happen?'

'I can't guarantee it, obviously, but I *can* get you off the gallows. However, I would need assistance from you, *after* you tell me what really happened.'

Ponsonby sighed. 'I've nothing to lose, have I?'

'Absolutely nothing, but a great deal to gain.'

'I suppose you know that it started with gambling debts?'

'Indeed, at Montague's, on an evening during which you were tempted into wagering more than you were good for, after consuming too many brandies.'

'You can blame that greasy von Huber for that,' Ponsonby growled. 'He pretended to befriend me, admiring my service record and my position as a royal valet. Then he bought me the best part of a bottle of brandy and invited me to play baccarat, with the club as banker, as was their normal arrangement. I was in for several thousand, and obviously couldn't honour the debt there and then, so my club membership was suspended, and I was terrified that my lapse would be reported to the prince. It would have been the end of my duties at the palace, because there can be no whiff of scandal surrounding anyone close to the throne, even though the prince himself is a walking scandal. But you don't need to know any of that.'

'Indeed not,' Percy concurred, 'although the prospect that you might make public revelations of *those* matters as a sort of "death cell confession" might nudge the prince even further towards intervening to keep you out of one. But please continue.'

'Well,' Ponsonby recalled with a long face, 'that rat von Huber contacted me a week or so after my suspension and intimated that I might be of possible service to him if he performed certain services for me. I agreed, partly because I could not see any other way out of my difficulties, and in the belief that he just wanted details regarding the prince's sexual exploits, which could fill an entire book.'

'And he paid your debts, then arranged for your club membership to be reinstated?'

'Correct. I began in a small way, giving von Huber a list of the society ladies who'd ended up in Prince Albert's bed. Then he told me that what I'd told him had been passed on to his superior, the German Kaiser, and he was anxious to learn more. It was at this point that von Huber really started to put the pressure on me, threatening to make the prince's peccadilloes public *and* reveal his source — me. That would also have been the end of my career.'

'So you were persuaded to take it a stage further, during the shooting party weekend at Bradenham House?'

'Yes. The original idea was for me to set the prince up for the murder of Lady Belvedere, allegedly when she threatened to reveal their affair to the public.'

'But there was no such affair, was there?' Percy objected.

Ponsonby shook his head. 'Not so far as I'm aware, but von Huber very cleverly planted seeds of doubt in Sir Rupert's head. What we hadn't bargained for was that Sir Rupert would enter the bedchamber with his wife. The plan was for her to go in alone, and for Prince Albert to be blindfolded while I shot her, then escaped via the adjoining dressing room. I was checking the window and loading my revolver earlier that day, when Sir Rupert's valet came in, insisting that *he* had been told to attend Prince Albert, and demanding to know what I was about. So I shot him there and then and hid his body, since this was only shortly after lunch, when the guns had started up again in the grouse woods.'

'You hid him in that linen chest inside the dressing room?'

'You really *have* investigated this case down to the last detail, haven't you?'

'Guilty as charged,' Percy agreed. 'What I *didn't* know was that the original target had been Lady Virginia.'

'Yes, well, it didn't work out that way,' Ponsonby replied ruefully. 'I was almost completely thrown when Sir Rupert came in, leading a blindfolded Lady Virginia, and saw me dragging the corpse of his valet into the bedchamber. I just reacted and shot him dead, then fired another one into the ceiling, to account for the two dead bodies. Of course, that left three empty chambers in the revolver, as you no doubt picked up on.'

'That was the first thing about the case that struck me as odd,' Percy told him. 'That, and the absence of the valet's blood on the carpet, suggesting to me that he'd been killed earlier. You then put the revolver down on the prince's bedside table, which you'd carefully placed on that side of the bed in advance, then beat a hasty retreat through the dressing room door, locking it from the other side. Have I missed anything, other than the fact that you sprained your ankle when you exited through the bathroom window? You were seen doing that by a witness, by the way.'

'No, you've got all the salient facts, damn you,' Ponsonby muttered. 'Now tell me how you can possibly weave all that into a story that will keep me from the public executioner.'

'Well, let's see now,' Percy mused. 'You'd been told that Wilson — that was the name of Sir Rupert's valet, by the way — was indisposed. Therefore, when you attended to the prince's blindfold, then saw Wilson coming through that adjoining door from a place he had no business to be, at the same time that Sir Rupert entered the bedchamber — seemingly holding his wife captive and blindfolded — you suspected some sort of plot against the prince. Your well-honed service instincts played you false and you let fly two shots, and given your skills with firearms they both hit their targets. You then panicked, dropped the revolver on the side table, ran through the dressing room into the bathroom and shinned down the drainpipe, spraining your ankle in the process.'

'But even in that version of events, I deliberately shot two people dead,' Ponsonby challenged him. 'That's still murder, isn't it?'

'No, it's an understandable misreading of the situation,' Percy countered. 'A piece of gross carelessness, of which you were so ashamed that you panicked and said nothing at the time. Then when the police came up with their ludicrous conclusion that the deaths were the result of a duel, you kept quiet, hoping that nothing more would come of it.'

'So if that's what the police have concluded, why am I now putting my hand up for the shootings?'

'Because your ill-chosen friend von Huber manipulated you into shooting two people dead in circumstances that could, at a pinch, be stretched to inculpate Prince Albert. As you're probably aware, the prince and his nephew the Kaiser are, shall we say, somewhat "distanced", and all the indications are that von Huber, when he wove his evil web, was acting on the direct orders of the Kaiser. That's why von Huber wormed his way into the company of one of Albert's society friends, looking for an opportunity to bring about a scandal that might suggest to the English establishment that the prince wasn't fit to rule. This would generate a constitutional crisis of which the Kaiser could take considerable advantage. You can now perhaps see more clearly why we need you to advise a court that you were the one who fired the shots, and why the English authorities might be well disposed towards letting you off the hook.'

'Quite,' Ponsonby replied with a nod. 'So what happens to me while you try to persuade the authorities to play along with your suggestion?'

'I'll have you transferred from here to Newgate,' Percy replied, 'where conditions are a little better than in this dreadful place. At least I can organise for you to have a cell to yourself. I take it that you'll cooperate?'

'Do I have a choice?'

'If I judge you accurately, you've already made that choice,' Percy replied pleasantly as he rose to leave.

'Out of the question!' Melville insisted hotly as Percy put his suggestion to him in the middle of that afternoon, at a meeting hastily convened in Bruce's office.

'Do you have any better ideas?' Percy replied, equally hotly. 'Let me remind you of what we were commissioned to achieve here. You wanted us to dig the heir to the English throne out of a double murder accusation, and we've achieved that, if only you'd take the starch out of your pride!'

'That's insubordination!' Melville all but screamed.

'It's common sense!' Percy retorted. 'Clearly you have to take this God-given opportunity to solve your diplomatic problem!' He rose angrily from his seat and stormed out, slamming the door behind him.

Jack squirmed in his chair, frozen with embarrassment, as Bruce asked him, 'What do you think, Jack?'

'I can't think of a better way of resolving the issue,' Jack admitted reluctantly. 'As Uncle Percy pointed out, with his customary lack of tact, our mission was to find evidence that exonerated Prince Albert. We've done that, and if we adopt his suggestion we can stifle any rumours that the Kaiser may already be circulating regarding who fired those shots. It's a far better resolution of the case than the unconvincing conclusion reached by the Buckinghamshire police, and we'd have testimony on the public record that proves on oath what actually happened. Why would a man plead guilty to something that might consign him to Newgate for a number of years, if it's not true? And Prince Albert could become our king as planned, the constitutional crisis would be avoided, and we'd have grounds for having von Huber sent back to Germany.'

Melville appeared to have calmed down as he observed, 'Put like that, it makes a good deal of sense.'

'But it's no different to what Uncle Percy said,' Jack reminded him.

'It was more a matter of how he put it,' Melville replied as he rose from his seat. 'I'll have a quick word with the Home Secretary and report back.'

After the door had closed behind him, Bruce gave a chuckle. 'You just learned a valuable lesson, Jack. It's not *what* you say, but how you say it. I want you to take over this case yourself, not just as the notional officer in charge, but as the actual rider of the horse. Go back down and await my call.'

CHAPTER SIXTEEN

Jack's first thought as he went back down to his own office was of where Percy might have got to after storming out of their meeting with Bruce and Melville. He made an anxious telephone call to Percy's business office, only to be told by the former police officer employed as Percy's general assistant that he hadn't seen Percy since the last time he'd been here, in company with Jack.

The clock seemed to be moving at half its normal speed as Jack sorted through paperwork that required his urgent attention, then nervously made his way to the house in Hackney via the overcrowded horse bus. There was a light on in the sitting room, and Jack pushed open the door to find Percy half slumped in his favourite armchair, a whisky bottle and glass on a side table nearby. He looked up dolefully as he saw Jack enter.

'If you want supper, you'll have to go out and get it,' he growled.

Jack heaved a sigh of relief to find his uncle still alive, and not yet comatose from liquor. 'What do you fancy?' he asked.

'Nothing at this moment, but the smell of a well cooked beef roast might revive my appetite,' Percy replied with a yawn.

Jack tactfully removed the whisky bottle and hid it in the broom cupboard, then lost no time in visiting the local cook shop that Percy normally favoured, bringing back a beef roast with accompanying vegetables. To his great relief, he discovered that Percy had roused himself and set the table. Jack smilingly laid the meal down in the centre, hoping that Percy's stomach would prove to be as susceptible as usual to the smell of a tempting meal. They began eating in silence, then Percy looked up to enquire, 'How did things end with Melville?'

'He left shortly after you did.'

'I really made a mess of things, didn't I?' Percy said gloomily.

Jack had never seen his uncle in such a state, and sought desperately for something to say that might lift his mood. 'Yes and no,' he began. 'You certainly ruffled Melville's feathers, but fortunately he could see the sense in what you were saying, and he undertook to contact the Home Secretary with your proposal.'

'Thank God!' Percy muttered as the trace of a smile became visible. 'I'd hate to think that Ponsonby might get away with it. But it might be better if you handle things on your own from now on.'

Jack sagged with relief as he realised that he wouldn't need to tactfully explain that Assistant Commissioner Bruce had left him in no doubt that he was to take matters forward alone, but he still had to step carefully around Percy's ego.

'If you say so, but I'll still need you behind the scenes to advise on tactics. We've got this far only because of your superior experience. I'll only keep going if you promise not to leave me hanging out to dry.'

'No, you can rest assured on that point, Jack,' Percy told him as the old grin returned, then he changed the subject. 'Do you think it might be safe to invite your aunt back here to survey the changes I've made? And do you *honestly* think that Annabelle will like it here?'

'Of course she will,' Jack reassured him. 'After all, *I* did, and there are all the distractions of the park across the road.'

It fell briefly silent, then Percy announced, 'I had in mind going back to Watford tomorrow and collecting your aunt, then bringing her back here. It's only three weeks until the Easter school holidays, and if there are major changes that need to be made here before we play host to Annabelle, then the sooner I'm advised the better.'

'That sounds like an excellent idea, Uncle,' Jack replied. 'I might come with you, since I've been missing home and family, and as far as I'm concerned the Yard owes me a day off. Could we make use of Jennings, do you think?'

'That's up to you, Jack. Jennings was allocated to us for the duration of the enquiry. If you can dream up some excuse for needing to go back to Watford, then we can do so in comfort, and without the need to ride that bone-shaker from Euston.'

'Well, given that Esther's been invaluable in double-thinking our every conclusion in the case, I think we might justify another consultation with her. If you've finished, let me wash up and tidy the kitchen ahead of the regal inspection by Aunt Beattie when you bring her back. Then I think we'll need an early night. What time does your assistant open your office in the morning? Only I'll need to make use of your telephone in order to get Jennings here tomorrow.'

'Why wait until then?' Percy asked. 'I'll go up there while you're washing up, and leave a message with Communications for him to be despatched first thing tomorrow. Then it's back to leafy Watford.'

A smiling Beattie met them at the front door of The Lodge shortly before noon the next day and offered to get Polly to prepare a hasty lunch for them all.

'How long are you here for this time?' Beattie asked drily over the omelettes that Alice placed in front of them all in the dining room.

Percy smiled as he replied, 'For long enough to take you back to Hackney, to survey the changes I've made ahead of Annabelle's holiday with us. I take it that this is still going to happen?'

'Of *course* it is,' Beattie insisted, 'and I can only hope that you'll make yourself available to show her the delights of Victoria Park. She's excited at the prospect of visiting the bathing pond, and she assures me that she wants to write a story about all the elves who live in the Chinese pagoda. She's developed quite an interest in writing as well as reading, so you'll need to indulge her by sitting and listening politely as she reads you her latest story, all of which seem to involve the "little people" who engage her imagination. I think she was intrigued by *The Princess and the Goblin*, which she insists on reading to me at least twice a week.'

'Jack's taken over the few remaining loose ends of that case we were working on,' Percy told her, 'so when we return home I'll be at your complete disposal to make whatever changes to the house and gardens you deem appropriate.'

'He's made quite a few already,' Jack added, 'and you'd hardly recognise my old room.'

'Let's hope not anyway, the state you used to get it into,' Beattie replied frostily, then insisted, 'I'm not leaving here today until I've had the opportunity to say goodbye to Annabelle, of course.'

Later that afternoon the family began returning home, beginning with a noisy and breathless Bertie, who claimed to have run all the way home from his Board school. 'I was being pursued by Boer infantry,' he explained. 'But I managed to outrun them, and once I reached the safety of the fort, the riflemen under my command sprayed them away.'

Jack shook his head sadly, and Percy chuckled as he told him, 'He reminds me of a young lad who once lived with us, who sailed his boat on the lake in the park, convinced that it was commanded by Admiral Nelson.'

Once Esther returned with Annabelle and Lily, Beattie lost no time in taking Annabelle into the sitting room, where Miriam and Tommy had been playing chess all afternoon, in accordance with their own rules. She told Annabelle that she and "Uncle Percy" were going back to their London house in order to make it ready for her holiday with them, and that she wanted Annabelle to write a story about her final few weeks at school and bring it with her when she came. Then she gave her a farewell kiss on the cheek and emerged from the sitting room with a tear in her eye.

'Let's waste no more time in idle gossip,' she instructed Percy. 'And don't even *think* of staying for supper, because that poor coachman you dragged up here has to get back to his family, and we've got a house to organise.'

Once Beattie and Percy had departed, Esther and Jack were left alone in the dining room. Over pre-dinner drinks, Esther asked how things were going in the Belvedere enquiry.

'It's all but completed, thanks to Uncle Percy's genius for not following the rules. Ponsonby — who you'll remember was the prince's valet who we suspected all along of being responsible for the deaths — made a frank confession. All that remains are the final details regarding the reduced sentence that we're hoping to offer him in return for his very public confession that he was responsible.'

'And he's been foolish enough to agree to that?' Esther asked. 'I had assumed that the man is intelligent.'

'He is,' Jack nodded. 'Intelligent enough to realise that what we really wanted was to quash any suggestion that Prince

Albert was the guilty party. Percy put a proposal to him which, if approved by the Home Secretary, will result in him getting a relatively mild prison sentence for pleading guilty to manslaughter, which is best described as "murder in mitigating circumstances." Once he does that, then the prince's name will be cleared, and the evil genius from the German Embassy who was behind it all will be expelled from England with his tail between his legs.'

'Excellent!' Esther murmured. 'Does this mean that you'll be home more often? Only we need to ensure that everything here is as good as it can be between now and August.'

'That's *months* away!' Jack objected. 'Why August?'

'Because that's when we go to court regarding Annabelle. The papers arrived yesterday, along with a letter from Launceston, our barrister.'

Two days later Jack was in the process of finalising a schedule of interviews with applicants for recruitment into the Met when his new assistant, Constable Venables, appeared in his doorway.

'A message from the Assistant Commissioner, sir. Very brief — in fact, only three words: "My office — now." Sounded pretty urgent, sir.'

Jack sighed and threw down his pen. 'Meetings with Bruce always are. I wonder if he gives his wife five minutes' notice when he wants his breakfast on the table.'

A few minutes later, Jack was standing in Bruce's office. There was a man seated in one of the interview chairs, who looked Jack up and down appraisingly.

'Close the door, then take a seat,' Bruce instructed Jack. After he'd done so, Bruce nodded towards the other visitor. 'You probably haven't met before, but this gentleman is Mr

Charles Ritchie, the Home Secretary. He's here to discuss your proposal for letting that Ponsonby chap off the hook.'

'It was actually Percy Enright's idea,' Jack replied modestly.

'But, as I recall, you agreed,' said Bruce. 'Since the other Enright is no longer on the case, it falls to you to justify what sounds like a travesty of justice unless fully explained. So go ahead and explain it fully.'

Jack took a deep breath and outlined the entire investigation, his and Percy's conclusions, and the deal they had made with Ponsonby. When he had finished, the Home Secretary was glaring at him.

'You're proposing a whitewash?' Ritchie challenged. 'A soft sentence in return for Ponsonby putting his hand up? A perversion of the usual justice process to achieve an outcome that suits you?'

'An outcome beneficial to the entire nation, sir,' Jack insisted.

'And why do you suggest that we in the Home Office should go along with it?' Ritchie demanded.

Jack could almost imagine Percy at his shoulder as he replied, 'In order to achieve what you sent us to achieve, sir. You requested that we find facts that absolved the heir to the throne, and we have. I'm a police officer, not a politician. It's now up to you what you do with the result. I can say no more than that.'

'And you've said enough,' Ritchie replied as he broke into a smile and rose from his seat, glancing down at Bruce before he turned towards the door. 'Excellent work, Bruce. This man is to be commended. And the other chap, whatever his name was. I'll lose no time in organising the next step.'

'I can only add my grateful thanks for a job well done, Jack,' Bruce said once the Home Secretary had left. 'You *and* Percy, who may now feel free to submit his account. I won't disclose the final figure to Melville, because I don't think his heart could survive it. Off you go, take a few days off whenever your normal duties permit, and let's see if we can recruit a few more like you into the Met, shall we?'

Back home, Jack was taking full advantage of Bruce's offer to let him catch up on his home life, and Esther was only too glad to have him back. She seemed to be as keen as Beattie had been to ensure that when they went to court in August, they'd have a good chance of being granted custody of Annabelle.

'Do you think they'll send someone from the court to inspect the house?' she asked nervously as they lay in bed, listening to the late spring rain bouncing off the roof tiles.

'I hardly think so,' Jack replied. 'From what Launceston told us, it's more a matter of proving that we're fit and proper people to be allowed the supervision of a young girl. Given that we've had four children of our own and none of them has come to any harm, if you discount Bertie's sprained ankle, I don't think we need concern ourselves on that score.'

'But suppose that this awful Mrs Drinkwater gets all sorts of influential people to produce testimonials, saying what a wonderful woman she is and how Annabelle would benefit greatly from the social advancement with which she can provide her? Do we know anyone who could testify regarding *our* virtues as parents?'

'I'll give it some thought,' said Jack. 'Now go to sleep.'

'I only wish I could,' Esther replied with a sob in her voice. 'I just lie awake thinking about the horrible possibility that Annabelle will be taken from us. I've grown to love her as much as our own children.'

Jack comforted her until he heard her breaths slowing and becoming deeper. Once she was asleep, he allowed himself to drift off.

Two days later, Jack's desk phone rang shrilly, jerking him out of his gloomy ruminations. He lifted the receiver and answered, 'Enright.'

'Is that *Chief Inspector* Enright?' asked the plummy-voiced caller. When Jack confirmed that it was, he was told, 'This is Giles Somerset from the Home Secretary's Office. The Home Secretary will pick you up in his coach at two o'clock today, at the Whitehall entrance to Scotland Yard. You'll be attending an audience with His Majesty, so please dress appropriately.'

At the appointed hour, the coach executed a wide turn in front of the ornamental brick entrance pillars of New Scotland Yard, and the coachman stepped down to open its doors for Jack to scurry inside. Awaiting him in its gloomy but well-padded interior was the Home Secretary, who shouted the instruction to 'move on' and then fixed Jack with a stern gaze.

'Any idea what this is about?' Ritchie asked.

'I was assuming that you'd be advising *me*, sir,' Jack replied.

'No bloody idea, and I have to be elsewhere,' Ritchie grumbled. 'I assume that it's a pat on the back for pulling him out of that compromising situation that he dropped himself into. You've heard the latest, presumably?'

'No, sir,' Jack told him truthfully.

'Well, it seems that Ponsonby has agreed to bite the bullet, so I've instructed the German Embassy that von Huber's no longer *persona grata* in England. The Foreign Secretary took it upon himself to advise the palace, no doubt seeking to steal my thunder, and I assume that the prince is awaiting a fuller report from the man who should have been allowed to break the news to him in the first place, namely myself. Since you know the precise circumstances that led to this welcome turn of events, I'm taking you with me to answer the awkward questions. You'll be dropped off back here afterwards.'

Ritchie then lapsed into a gloomy silence, glancing anxiously at his fob watch at least three times during the short journey up Whitehall, then down The Mall to the palace. There they were escorted along the same internal route that Jack remembered from his last visit, and were ushered into the presence.

'Ah, Ritchie, thanks for coming,' the prince smiled broadly, 'and for bringing this young fellow, who from memory was the one who was smoking out that wretched Ponsonby. At least the slimy rotter decided to do the decent thing, thanks to you, young man. Tell me how that came about.'

'If I might be permitted to withdraw, Your Majesty?' Ritchie requested. 'I'm due at a Cabinet meeting that began two minutes ago in Downing Street.'

'Not until you assure me that von Huber's left the country,' Prince Albert insisted.

Ritchie smiled. 'He took the night ferry to Paris two nights ago, Your Majesty, after the German Ambassador was left in no doubt that we regarded the man's illicit activities as unworthy of someone privileged to have been granted diplomatic immunity. We also sent a copy of our letter of protest to the German Chancery in Berlin, for the personal attention of your nephew the Kaiser.'

'Excellent!' Prince Albert chuckled. 'Anyway, you may go, Ritchie, but leave the young fellow with me.'

'Sit down, young man,' Prince Albert invited Jack. 'I remember your face, but I can't remember your name.'

'Enright, Your Majesty. Chief Inspector Jack Enright.'

'Quite. But you had an older chap with you last time, didn't you? The one who did all the talking?'

'That was my uncle, Percy Enright, Your Majesty.'

'And now you can speak for both of you, I assume?'

'I can indeed, Your Majesty.'

'No need to add my title to every reply, young man,' said the prince, smiling, 'since I know who I am without having to be reminded every five seconds. Now, how did you persuade Ponsonby to drop his trousers, so to speak?'

'We offered him what is vulgarly called "a deal", Your — sorry. Our primary aim was to prove that you hadn't fired those shots, and the best way to do that was to identify the one who had. We told Ponsonby that if he admitted to it, we'd arrange for what should have been a murder charge to become a lesser one, and his sentence would probably not exceed five years.'

'A bit *infra dig*, wasn't it? And don't you police chaps like to get the maximum sentence for crimes, in order to discourage the others?'

'Ordinarily, yes,' Jack conceded. 'But we considered that your orderly succession to the throne was more valuable than seeing a man take the drop at Newgate. And no-one else is likely to be encouraged to set you up for something you didn't do, so there's no need for a deterrent in this case.'

'Very patriotic, and I can just imagine, at this point, my mother ordering tea and scones. But I could probably do better than that. Perhaps some sort of honour?'

'That would be very generous of you, but perhaps excessive, in view of the fact that we were only doing our job.'

'But there must be *something* I can do in return for your excellent service to me?'

A memory of Esther's distraught face when informed of the forthcoming court date flashed across Jack's mind. 'As a matter of fact there is, if it wouldn't be too presumptuous of me.'

CHAPTER SEVENTEEN

On a day in mid-August that they'd been dreading, the entire Enright family walked down the long entrance hall of the Court of Chancery. For Jack and Percy, it was their second court attendance in a matter of months.

The first had been at the Old Bailey, to which Ponsonby's trial had been transferred in late May on the authority of the Director of Public Prosecutions. It had not been a trial as such, since Ponsonby was, with the consent of the senior prosecutor allocated to the matter, pleading guilty to two charges of manslaughter. The prosecutor went no further than advising the judge who would be passing sentence in due course that the deaths of Sir Rupert Belvedere and his valet James Wilson had been the result of a 'tragic misjudgement on the part of the prisoner in what he believed to be an impending assassination attack upon his master.' The precise identity of that master was tactfully omitted, and at the end of his startlingly short address to the Bench, the prosecutor concluded by advising his lordship that he and the defence counsel agreed that a sentence of five years' imprisonment would adequately reflect the charges.

It was then the turn of defence counsel to advise the judge of his client's distinguished career as an officer of the Coldstream Guards, one that had encompassed a period as Adjutant to the Constable of the Tower of London, and service inside the royal palaces as a personal valet to the man who would shortly become the new king. 'His promising career has obviously been sacrificed as the result of what at worst might be described as a moment of gross negligence in the performance of his duties, and at best as the actions of a man devoted to the service of his master,' the defence counsel went on. 'He is naturally most remorseful of his actions, and can only bow his head in shame as he awaits whatever sentence your lordship deems appropriate. As my learned friend has indicated, we are *ad idem* in our opinion that a period of five years would be an adequate reflection, not only of the seriousness of my client's crimes, but of the tragic circumstances in which they occurred. Unless there is anything else I can assist the court with, your lordship, those are my submissions.'

Mr Justice Melbury had been briefed in advance not to enquire as to the identity of the 'master' whose life Ponsonby had believed himself to be defending, and that if the two counsel came up with an appropriate sentence, then justice might best be seen to be served if he passed a sentence in agreement with that. Ponsonby duly received a five-year sentence. He smiled as he thanked the judge, then scowled at Jack and Percy as he was being led back down to the cells beneath the courtroom.

This time, however, the outcome was far from pre-determined, and the Enrights nervously took their places on the long bench inside Courtroom No 2 of the Chancery Court, behind their counsel, Spencer Launceston. On the other benches to their left sat a stern-faced woman who Annabelle had barely acknowledged as she waved to her. In a whisper to Beattie, seated on her left, Annabelle identified the woman as her aunt, Rose Drinkwater. The lady was accompanied by a man who looked as if he would rather be anywhere other than where he was, and who was in turn identified by Annabelle as her 'horrible Uncle Thomas.'

After a delay of only a few minutes, the door to the rear of the Bench opened to admit Mr Justice Greenwood of the

Court of Chancery. He bowed solemnly to the two counsel who had risen at his entrance, and invited 'Mr Strong, for the Petitioner,' to make his opening address.

The Enrights had been told by Launceston that the proceedings to which they had been summoned as the 'Respondents' did not take the form of an ordinary trial. Instead, each of the parties would make submissions, produce relevant documents, and argue their case for custody of the 'minor child', as Annabelle was described for present purposes. She snuggled into Beattie's shoulder, with Esther on her other side holding her hand comfortingly, as James Strong KC outlined his arguments for custody of Annabelle to be granted to his client.

'Following certain tragic events with which I need not trouble your lordship, Mrs Rose Drinkwater is the minor child's only surviving relative,' he said. 'As your lordship is well aware, the familial claim is always considered the most meritorious in the absence of any compelling counter-argument.'

He went on to emphasise Thomas Drinkwater's status as a solicitor, his respected standing in the local Cheltenham community, his membership of various local charitable organisations, and his almost lifetime attendance at the local Anglican church. This provoked a snort of derision from Beattie that she stifled in her glove, and which fortunately was not audible from the Bench. She contained her rising temper as she heard Strong describe the current arrangements under which Annabelle was living.

'The situation is somewhat precarious, and dependent solely on the charitable motivations of her school teacher, the Respondent Mrs Esther Enright, who took the girl in initially so as to preserve her from an orphanage. As your lordship will readily appreciate, ties that are not familial in origin can never be relied upon to continue, and the family with which the minor child currently resides already contains four children, ranging in age from eleven to five. It is arguably a considerable financial burden for a family that already contains four children to make room for a fifth, and should their fortunes decline for any reason in the future, then naturally they could be expected to give preference to their own flesh and blood.'

Strong concluded by filing a bundle of testimonials from local worthies from Cheltenham, all of whom spoke of the respectability and good name of the Drinkwaters. The judge then opted to take a mid-morning break.

'He made out a strong case for the Drinkwaters,' Esther observed with a long face as they sat in the hallway outside the courtroom, 'whereas he made us sound like some tinker family who barely had enough money to scrape together to feed the children we already had.'

'Don't allow yourself to get despondent at this stage,' Launceston urged her. 'His lordship has only heard one side of the overall picture. When he hears what I have to say — and in particular the character references that Jack has put together — the decision that his lordship has to make will appear much more evenly balanced. And, as I already told you, Greenwood has developed this practice, which other Chancery judges seem to be following, of speaking to the child regarding how they wish their future to proceed. Annabelle must be prepared to make it clear that she wants to stay with your family.'

'Of *course* I will,' Annabelle piped up, 'but if that judge sends me to live with Aunt Rose, I'll just ran back to the circus.'

'I strongly recommend that you don't say that to the judge,' Launceston said with a grin. Then he looked up as the courtroom door opened, and the judge's bailiff beckoned the parties back inside.

It was now Launceston's turn. He laboured at some length over the circumstances that had led Annabelle to run away from her natural mother and her 'demeaning' stepfather to join a travelling circus, from which she'd been rescued by 'the two male Enright Respondents', at the request of Mrs Esther Enright.

'Mrs Enright has for the past two years and more been the schoolteacher of the minor child, and offered her a new home when her stepfather murdered her mother, and was subsequently hanged,' he said. 'It says much for the new home environment in which the minor child has been subsequently raised by the Respondents Jackson and Esther Enright — a loving home that I have been privileged to visit for myself — that the child has blossomed from being a shy, withdrawn and thoroughly dispirited product of a demeaning so-called family, and today presents as a cheerful, obedient and well-educated child. Her future, had she not been taken in by the Respondents, would have been sadly predictable, and one of which your lordship hears daily in this court.

'There is an additional factor to be woven into the decision that ultimately falls upon your lordship to make, namely the interest shown in the child by the uncle and aunt of the Respondent Jackson Enright. Percy Enright, the uncle, has retired after a long and meritorious career as an inspector in Scotland Yard, and is now living the quiet life that he has earned with his religious, generous and loving wife Beatrice. The senior Enrights are childless, your lordship, but possessed of a spacious house in Hackney, across the road from Victoria Park, to which they wish to welcome the minor child during her school holidays. There is a noticeable bond already formed between Beatrice Enright and Annabelle, which is best described as that of "child and favourite aunt", and it has been largely under the benign and encouraging wing of that lady that the minor child has begun to develop an interest in literary matters that far exceeds that which might be expected in a child of nine.

'As for the family's financial circumstances, I can advise your lordship that Jackson Enright is a Chief Inspector of Police with Scotland Yard, where he is responsible for all recruitment into the Metropolitan Police, while his wife Esther Enright is the Deputy Headmistress of Cassiobury House private school in Watford, which, as I've already indicated, is attended by the minor child. Both Respondents enjoy careers that are well shielded from the economic vagaries of other means of livelihood, and on several visits to their spacious family home I've detected no indications of poverty, or indeed any financial stress whatsoever.

'Finally, the matter of personal testimonials. I have both confidence and pleasure in filing, for your lordship's consideration, a series of such that include one from Miss Emily Allsop, proprietor and headmistress of Cassiobury House School, the Reverend William Glossop, the resident minister of Hackney Methodist Mission, and Assistant Commissioner Bruce of Scotland Yard. Then there is one more, which your lordship might find of a particularly persuasive quality.'

Launceston lifted two large sealed envelopes from the bar table at which he was standing, and slid one across to Strong. Strong opened it, gasped in amazement, and handed it to a speechless instructing solicitor, who in turn passed it back to Mrs Drinkwater. She emitted a groan and let her chin droop onto her chest. The judge had watched this little pantomime with some interest, and he looked down at Launceston with the hint of a smile.

'This document would seem to have some bearing on the case,' he said drily as he held out his hand. His bailiff walked to where Launceston was standing, took the envelope from him and handed it up to the judge.

As he was in the process of opening it, Launceston observed, 'You will see, if you read the signature, that it would perhaps be in the best interests of these proceedings if the identity of the signatory to this final testimonial were to remain undisclosed in open court.'

'Indeed,' the judge muttered as his eyebrows shot up and threatened to become part of his wig. 'I've seen a few remarkable testimonials in my time, but never — well, never one from *this* source. Do you have any further submissions, Mr Launceston?'

'No, your lordship. Perhaps in view of the time?'

'Yes, quite. Close the court, Mr Bailiff, but have the minor child attend me in my chambers at two o'clock, along with the female Respondent.'

'What happens now?' Esther asked nervously as they stood in a group on the courthouse steps, keen to take in some of the warm summer sunshine, but too nervous to require any lunch. Even Percy declared himself not to be hungry.

'Annabelle and yourself will be admitted to the judge's private chambers at two o'clock,' Launceston told them, 'and he'll have a little chat with Annabelle about what *she* wants. I'm not saying that it will be decisive, but clearly she needs to impress upon his lordship that she wants to stay with you in Watford, taking her holidays in Hackney.'

'I don't think she'll leave him in any doubt about that,' Esther said with a chuckle.

As St Paul's "Great Tom" bell to the east rang out two o'clock in the afternoon, Esther and Annabelle were ushered into the judge's chambers by his ever-present bailiff, and Percy insisted on going back outside to stand on the steps and light his pipe. Jack joined him, and they stood nervously surveying the passing traffic, amongst which were a small number of the latest toys of the rich and influential — 'horseless carriages', which banged and spluttered their way up and down The Strand.

'Noisy buggers, aren't they?' Percy commented. 'And they create such a stink!'

'Almost as bad as your pipe,' Jack observed as he changed sides in order to get upwind of it.

After what felt like an hour, but was in fact less than half of that, Launceston appeared at the top of the steps and beckoned them back inside. 'His lordship wants us back in there by three-thirty,' he announced.

'How did things go in the judge's private room?' Jack asked anxiously.

Launceston smiled. 'Ask Esther. She was almost beside herself with pleasure, and she's taken Annabelle in search of a ladies' convenience.'

They resumed their seats outside the courtroom, where they were joined shortly afterwards by a beaming Esther and Annabelle.

'Annabelle was *so* good in there!' Esther enthused. 'I swear she'll be a wonderful little actress one day — she charmed the old man to pieces! Mind you, he *was* very kind and gentle with her, and she seemed to take to him. And she never once mentioned running away to the circus!'

'I just told him how happy I was staying with you all in Watford,' Annabelle added, 'and how I can't wait to see the park where Aunt Beattie lives, and visit the Chinese house.'

'Why is the judge keeping us waiting until half past three?' Percy asked.

'I think he's going to deliver an *ex tempore* ruling,' Launceston replied. 'Sorry, I mean that he'll give us the gist of his decision verbally, ahead of preparing a more detailed written judgment. And judging by the looks on the faces of the opposition, I think we might afford to raise our hopes slightly.'

The Enright clan all but ran to reoccupy their benches when the bailiff opened the doors to them shortly before three-thirty, and shot to their feet when the judge resumed his seat on the Bench. He was clutching two sheets of paper, from which he read out loud as everyone resumed their seats.

'I've taken great care to listen to all the arguments urged upon me in this matter, and in accordance with the duty imposed upon me by the law of this country, I've placed particular importance on the wishes of the minor child. On the one hand, I have the excellent prospects afforded by the possibility that the child be restored to her remaining legal family member, the Petitioner, Mrs Drinkwater. There can be little doubt that were the minor child to be consigned to her care and custody, she would be raised in a modestly wealthy, professional, and respectable household, and one in which no-one might object to her becoming resident.

'On the other side of the equation, if I might call it that, is the household in which she is currently being raised. It is, by all the evidence made available to me, an equally respectable and professional one in which she has already established friendships with what might be termed her "step-siblings". There can be no doubt of the genuine love and care for her welfare that is being bestowed upon her, most notably by the two Enright ladies, Esther and Beatrice, who have a proposal to share access to her on the basis of the calendar of the school that she attends. I am satisfied that the current arrangements for her welfare have been such that she has thrived, and my brief conversation with her in chambers has left me in no doubt that she values the current arrangement, and is mindful of the kindness and love that has been shown to her.

'Were it simply a matter of comparing one household with another, my decision might have been harder to make. But as it is, I was very taken by the minor child herself when she described how much she wishes to maintain the *status quo*. Also bearing in mind that the guiding principle of the legislation by which I'm governed is the ultimate welfare of the minor child, it is with considerable confidence that I enter judgment for the Respondents. There will be no costs awarded in the matter, given the merits of the two submissions. Thank you for your attendance, and please close the court, Mr Bailiff.'

There was a stunned silence as everyone rose and bowed. As soon as the door behind the Bench had closed, Esther grabbed hold of Launceston's court gown and asked, with tears rolling down her face, 'Did that mean what I *hope* it meant?'

'It did indeed,' Launceston assured her. 'Annabelle will remain with you.'

'Thank God!' Esther bawled as she broke into loud sobs and threw herself into Jack's arms.

Beattie had remained in her seat, and was weeping quietly as Annabelle snuggled up to her and whispered, 'Please don't cry, Aunt Beattie — it's what I wanted.'

'It's what we *all* wanted, you dear, dear child,' Beattie choked as she buried her face in Annabelle's shoulder. Jack continued to hold a still sobbing Esther in his arms, then looked in vain for Percy to come and do the same for Beattie.

While the rest of the family were gathered around Launceston to thank him profusely for his services — Annabelle stepping on tiptoe to instruct him to lean down for a kiss on the cheek — Jack went outside in search of Percy. He found him on the courthouse steps, pipe clenched firmly in his mouth, with tears rolling down his cheeks.

'Damned cold wind goes for the eyes,' he complained, and Jack maintained a tactful silence.

'Mrs Drinkwater must be very sad,' he observed after a while.

'You think so?' Percy growled back. 'She passed me on the way out and told me — and I quote — "You're bloody welcome to my sister's brat." *That's* how sad she was.'

'Well, it worked out well in the end,' said Jack. 'For a while there I was genuinely fearful that we'd lose Annabelle, and we have *so* much we can give her, between us.'

'A life with the Enrights,' Percy said with a smile, his tears drying rapidly in the afternoon sun. 'Never dull, never "normal", never predictable. But you really went further than any Enright has ever done, my boy. I bet no-one else has ever entered a court of law armed with a personal testimonial from the king. I think that may have been my last case, Jack.'

'I'll believe that when that statue on the courthouse roof comes to life,' Jack replied with a chuckle, 'and even if it does, I'll need you beside me to advise me what to charge it with.'

A NOTE TO THE READER

Dear Reader,

Thank you for reading this new novel in the Enright series. I hope that it lived up to your expectations.

As ever, I drew upon the recorded historical events that dominated 1901, with the death of the long-reigning Queen Victoria and the accession of her eldest male heir, Prince Albert Edward, known to everyone — including many of his subjects — simply as 'Bertie'. If the ardent monarchists among my readers took exception to what they considered to be my gross exaggeration of the man's failings, then I point simply to the public record in my defence.

Bertie had been a problem even as a child, when he proved himself to be a poor scholar, and intolerant of the restraints imposed upon him by his parents in the hope that he would one day become the perfect product of a family seeking to establish itself as a respectable upper-middle-class role model for their subjects to follow. Victoria always blamed him for the death of his father, who caught a chill after walking in the rain with his errant son, devastated by the revelation that Bertie had lost his virginity to an 'actress' provided for him by his fun-loving army friends.

The immediate solution for his libidinous inclinations seemed to be an early marriage, and in 1863 his mother secured for him the hand of the elegant and beautiful Princess Alexandra of Denmark. They set up their London home in Marlborough House, and Bertie acquired Sandringham House in Norfolk as their country retreat. Both of these residences, but Marlborough House in particular, rapidly acquired a reputation for luxurious, extravagant and licentious parties, with the royal bride seemingly as enthusiastic as her husband to be a member of what became known as the 'Marlborough House Set', listing among its members some of the wealthiest and best-known 'worthies' of English society at that time.

They ate, drank and 'socialised' with enthusiasm and regularity, while the list of Bertie's rumoured sexual conquests read almost like a 'Who's Who' of English society at that time, and included actress Lily Langtry, Lady Randolph Churchill, the Countess of Warwick, actress Sarah Bernhardt and Alice Keppel, whose great granddaughter is now Queen Camilla. It seems that Alexandra turned a blind eye to these alleged liaisons that somehow seemed to endear Bertie to his subjects, to whom he presented as a loveable 'Jack the Lad', with a genial disposition and a love of life.

I did not invent the fragile relationship between Bertie and his irascible nephew, Kaiser Wilhelm of Germany. While Bertie was fun-loving and outgoing, Wilhelm was brittle, withdrawn, quick to take offence and envious of the love and admiration that his uncle always seemed to attract. They constantly competed with each other in a variety of contexts, most noticeably yacht-racing. The incident between them alluded to in this book, in which Bertie punched Wilhelm in the mouth following his loss to him at their annual Cowes race competition, is supported by word-of-mouth accounts handed down by those who were there when it happened. To make matters worse, Wilhelm's Prussian forebears had, at around the time of Alexandra's wedding to Bertie, seized Schleswig-Hostein from Denmark, and she always resented him as a result. It was no exaggeration to fictionalise, as I did, a petulant attempt by Wilhelm to prevent his detested uncle from ascending the throne of England.

Bertie was larger than life in more senses than one. His hedonistic lifestyle left him with a 122cm waistline by the date of his coronation, and he was rarely seen without a cigar in his mouth. This unhealthy lifestyle ensured that he enjoyed only nine years on the throne, dying in 1910 well before his seventieth birthday.

During this same period, the rivalry between Bertie and Wilhelm somehow became a rivalry between their two nations, and would, during the reign of Bertie's son, George V, explode into World War One. During Bertie's years, as suggested in the chapters you have read, the rivalry was industrial rather than military, although the underlying imperative seems to have been the development of powerful military forces with which to threaten each other. The competition for an improved steel-making process that gave the fictional von Huber his lever over the equally fictional Belvedere was a good case in point.

Other references within the novel call for additional background explanation. First of all, there is the incident referred to in Chapter One, in which Queen Victoria's coffin was almost lost from the gun carriage on which it was mounted when the horses detailed to pull it became restless. This incident really occurred: the horses, restless due to lack of exercise, reared up when the coffin was ceremonially loaded onto the gun carriage they had been detailed to pull. In an effort to save what could have been a highly embarrassing jettisoning of the coffin onto the ground, Prince Louis of Battenberg, married to one of Victoria's granddaughters, asked the Royal Navy party commander, Lieutenant Algernon Boyle, to assign a team of his sailors to pull the carriage using improvised drag ropes made from the horse harnesses. This was the origin of the very colourful tradition evident at all subsequent state funerals, when muscular naval ratings in dark clothing become human carriage haulers.

Secondly, I refer to the absence of any fingerprints on the obvious murder weapon. In 1901 this basic element of any contemporary forensic crime scene investigation was in its infancy, although the individuality of the 'loops and whorls' at the end of the human finger that made them unique to every person had been known since ancient times. By 1892 it had become a matter of academic interest, when Sir Franci Galton published a groundbreaking book entitled *Fingerprints*, which suggested a method by which they could be classified. This was developed by Sir Edward Henry into what became known as the Henry Classification System, widely adopted by leading police forces. Initially, in England, it was merely a means of indicating the identity of an offender, but in 1903 it was successfully employed to obtain a conviction in a minor burglary case, before leaping to public prominence two years later, when it secured the murder conviction of a man who left his 'dabs' on a money box while robbing, and bludgeoning to death, a local shopkeeper. It would certainly have assisted the police in our fictional case had the revolver butt been found to bear fingerprints.

Next, the child welfare provisions I described that decided future of little Annabelle Pickering were all historically accurate. The Church of England most certainly maintained a network of 'Moral Welfare Associations' that were integral to its self-imposed mission to address social issues, most notably those of prostitution, venereal diseases, and the welfare of unmarried mothers. They aimed to provide practical support and moral guidance, and offered shelter and support to women in need, while promoting sexual education and advocating for moral standards in society. While they may appear patronising to our modern eyes, it must be remembered that in the final years of the nineteenth century there was no public health service, no welfare state, and no legislative framework to protect the vulnerable.

One of the first to achieve that was the Prevention of Cruelty to, and Protection of, Children Act, enacted in 1889, under which Jack narrowly escaped being prosecuted for his son Bertie's sprained ankle and Annabelle's stint in the circus. The provisions cited in the chapter you have just read were accurately reproduced, and might be regarded as the first signs that the vulnerability of children in Victorian England was being recognised.

Finally, I refer to the Custody of Infants Act, 1873, under which Annabelle's aunt was able to 'petition' for custody of her niece. Until this legislation was enacted, only a parent could petition for custody of a natural child, but this was not always in the best interests of that child. This Act introduced two important new provisions: the first was that close relatives *other* than a parent could petition for custody, and the second was that priority was to be given to the best interests of the child. As indicated in this novel, it therefore became possible for a 'minor child' such as Annabelle to be allowed to remain where they were currently residing, against even the wishes of a close relative, if the judge deemed that it was in their 'best interests' to do so.

As ever, I would be delighted to see a review of my book posted on **Amazon** or **Goodreads**. Alternatively, feel free to visit, and contact me on, my author website: **davidfieldauthor.com**.

Happy reading!

David

Sapere Books is an exciting new publisher of brilliant fiction and popular history.

To find out more about our latest releases and our monthly bargain books visit our website:
saperebooks.com